CROSS YOUR HEART

"Are you jealous?" he asks me.

"Jealous?"

Gary smiles.

"Good," he says. "Because you haven't got anything to be jealous about."

"I don't?"

"I saved all my best stuff for you," he says. "Come here, and I'll show you."

He reaches out and grabs my hand and tries to pull me down to the bed with him, but I hold back.

"You said you loved me," I remind him.

"I do," he says. "I love you."

"Only?" I ask him.

"Only," he says, "and always."

I search his eyes, as if I could see into his heart. Is he lying to me?

"Convince me," I tell him.

Cross Your Heart

Bruce and Carole Hart

AN AVON  FLARE BOOK

AVON BOOKS
A division of
The Hearst Corporation
105 Madison Avenue
New York, New York 10016

Copyright © 1988 by The Laughing Willow Company, Inc.
Front cover photograph by Abe Rezny
Published by arrangement with The Laughing Willow Company, Inc.,
and International Creative Management, Inc.
Library of Congress Catalog Card Number: 87-91465
ISBN: 0-380-89971-X
RL: 4.6

First Avon Flare Printing: June 1988

AVON FLARE TRADEMARK REG. U.S. PAT. OFF. AND IN OTHER COUNTRIES, MARCA REGISTRADA.

Printed in Canada

UNV 10 9 8 7 6 5 4 3 2

One

You might have heard of me, Angelica Pierce. I was all over the news last summer, in the papers, and on TV. It was my fifteen seconds of fame. I was the teenager in the story that began "Teenager Breaks Up Million Dollar Drug Ring."

Except that wasn't really where the story began. It was more like where it ended. Where it began was one Saturday night, last April.

It was a warm spring night, maybe the first of the year, and I was working behind the candy counter at the Olympic Theatre. It was a weekend job that I'd taken so I could make some money to go to college, which is my mother's Master Plan for my future.

I want to go to college, too, of course, if only to get out of Waterford, which is *my* Master Plan for my future. Because, face it, if you don't get out of Waterford, which is about seventy miles due north of Syracuse, New York, and about as close as you can get to nowhere, there *is* no future.

Which isn't to say that Waterford isn't a nice place to grow up in. It's just that, if you want to do anything with your life, it's a better place to grow out of.

But anyway, that's where all this happened. My

breaking up of this million dollar drug ring and everything.

Except I'm pretty sure that the police or the papers must have exaggerated the size of the drug ring, which I guess they usually do, just to get people's attention. So it was probably more like a half-million dollar drug ring or quarter-million dollar drug ring or something. But you can see how that sounds a lot less impressive.

But anyway, the plan that night was, after the second show got started and I closed up the candy counter and turned over the money I'd taken in to Mr. Schwed, who runs the Olympic, I was supposed to sit down with my friends, Marlene and Janice and Toby and Gayle, who'd come to see the movie and were saving a seat for me, and watch the rest of the movie with them.

And then, after the movie was over, we were all supposed to pile into Marlene's Toyota and drive back to her house and watch *Saturday Night Live* together, even though it was a rerun that night and most of us had already seen it before.

The point was, it was Saturday night and none of us had dates, and nobody wanted to go home too early because it was Saturday night.

But anyway, that was the plan. Except Dwyer screwed it up.

Leave it to Dwyer. He came into the theatre with his regular gang—Boynton, Sullivan, Lazarus, and Bennett—about five minutes after Marlene and the others had taken their seats.

I can't stand Dwyer. I can't stand him now and I couldn't stand him then, because for one thing, at the time, he was supposed to be going out with Marlene, who was my best friend and who was really in love with him.

2

Except that didn't stop Dwyer, who thought he was God's gift to women, from making passes at all of Marlene's friends. Including me.

Only I didn't go for it. Although I suspected that Janice and a couple of the others had. But that was their business.

But anyway, there I was behind the candy counter, doing my dirty work for the dental profession, when in walks Dwyer. He walks up to the counter.

I say, "Can I help you?"

Dwyer gives me this disgusting I'm-gonna'-get-ya' smile of his and he says, "Could you ever."

Typical Dwyer.

I want to barf. But instead, I just say, "Plain or buttered?" and sell him a large buttercorn and off he goes with his motley crew.

The next thing I know, I'm cashing in and Toby's back at the candy counter, telling me that Dwyer and his gang have taken seats right behind them on the left side of the theatre about halfway down the aisle.

Which stinks because if I sit with Marlene and Janice and everybody, like we planned, there's no way I'm going to be able to concentrate on the movie. Not with Dwyer and his buddies sitting right behind me, wisecracking and horsing around, straight through the whole thing.

And the thing is, I like movies. I maybe even love them—movies and plays and novels—because as far as I'm concerned, the different worlds that people make up for us in movies and plays and novels have it all over the world that we actually live in.

And this movie in particular, *Blue Velvet*, I'm

3

really curious about because it doesn't sound like any movie I've ever heard of before.

The music sounds like the music you'd hear in one of those old black-and-white movies that they show on TV Saturday afternoons when the ball game's been rained out—kind of corny and old-fashioned.

But the rest of what you hear sounds more like one of those XXX movies that they advertise on the neon sign in front of The Gilded Cage Motel out on Route 8—with all this, you know, moaning and gasping and heavy breathing and everything.

And all day now, since just before one o'clock, I've been stuck behind the candy counter, listening to this half-corny/half-horny soundtrack. And as hard as I've tried, I still can't imagine what kind of picture the soundtrack could go with.

So, like I said, I'm really curious about it, which is why, when I've finished cashing in with Mr. Schwed, instead of looking for Marlene and everybody, I just find myself a seat at the back of the theatre—where I can really watch the picture—and plop myself down.

I won't tell you what *Blue Velvet* turns out to be about, in case you haven't seen it. But I will tell you that it blew me away.

Do you know what it's like when you have a really powerful dream and you wake up and you can't quite shake it off? How you're in a kind of daze—where you're definitely not sleeping anymore but you're not quite awake yet, either? Well, when *Blue Velvet* is over, that's how I feel.

I see Marlene and Janice and everybody coming up the aisle toward me—with Dwyer and his bunch trailing close behind them—but I'm in a daze.

I join up with them and walk out to the back of

4

the theatre with them. I see Mr. Schwed opening the doors to the lobby and letting out the crowd.
But the whole time, it's like I'm sleepwalking.

I'm kind of drifting toward the door, when I hear
Mr. Schwed say, "How'd you like it?"

As dreamy as I am, it takes me a second to figure
out who he's talking to and what he's talking about.
But then I remember that Mr. Schwed is always
asking me what I think of whatever movie we're
showing because he thinks that I'm a typical
teenager and he can figure out from my typical
teenager's reaction exactly how popular the movie's
going to be with the high school crowd.

But while my brain is still busy figuring all of this
out, I hear my mouth answering Mr. Schwed's
question. "A lot," it says.

I'm kind of surprised to hear my mouth talking
before I tell it to, but Mr. Schwed doesn't seem to
notice. He just smiles at me and looks over at the
crowd I'm with.

"How about your friends?" he says.

Gayle makes a face like she just ate a spoiled
clam. "It's too weird," she says.

"What was that he had in the mask?" asks
Toby.

"Oxygen," says Marlene.

"Nitrous," says Lazarus, chiming in where he
wasn't invited.

Lazarus and Dwyer and the rest of them have
kind of attached themselves to us by now. They're
hanging back a little way from us, but they're
definitely attached.

"Nitrous?" asks Mr. Schwed.

Lazarus nods and says, "Nitrous oxide. Like you
get at the dentist."

5

"I don't get anything at the dentist," says Dwyer.

My hero!

"I get felt up," says Janice.

Jesus!

Everybody cracks up, of course. Except for Mr. Schwed and me.

Mr. Schwed's mouth drops open, and I finally snap out of my daze.

I say a fast "good night and see you tomorrow" to Mr. Schwed, and I head for the door.

As I hit the lobby, I can hear Marlene and the gang giggling and laughing right behind me and—although I don't turn around to look—I imagine that Dwyer and his gang are right behind them. But when I hit the street and turn around to look for Marlene, I see that she's still back in the lobby, paired up with Dwyer and straggling behind.

So we wait—me and Janice and Toby and Gayle and Boynton and Sullivan and Lazarus and Bennett—we stand on the sidewalk outside the theatre and wait for Dwyer and Marlene to come out the door.

Finally they do and, as they do, Dwyer says to Marlene, "So where you headed now?"

Marlene shrugs, as if she didn't know.

"I don't know," she says, and then, as if she's making it up on the spot, she adds, "Probably just back to my house."

"We're going to watch *Saturday Night Live*," says Janice.

The way she says it, she makes it sound like watching *Saturday Night Live* is going to be the thrill of a lifetime.

But Sullivan doesn't share her enthusiasm.

"It's a rerun this week," he says.

Bennett nods.

"Robin Williams," he says.

"I saw it," says Lazarus.

"Me, too," says Boynton.

"Where are you headed?" Marlene asks Dwyer.

Dwyer shrugs.

"Oh," he says, "probably just back to your house."

Marlene laughs.

So does Janice.

I wonder how far Janice has gone with Dwyer and how far she plans to go.

"Is anybody home?" asks Dwyer.

"Just my parents," says Marlene. "And they're probably fast asleep by now, like they usually are."

Dwyer smiles at Marlene, and then he looks over at me.

"Is everybody coming?" he says, looking right at me.

"Yes," says Janice, as if Dwyer were looking at her.

God! She's so obvious!

"I can't," I say.

Bennett gets this funny look, as if he were disappointed.

Bennett?! That settles it.

"I've got to get home," I say.

"Aw, come on!" says Dwyer. "It's Saturday night!"

"Dead from New York," I remind him.

He laughs.

"It's not like your mother's waiting up for you," he says.

I don't say anything.

He says, "She's still working at the country club, isn't she?"

7

"Yes," I tell him.

My mother's a legal secretary during the week, but weekends she works as the hostess in the dining room at the Pinebrook Golf and Country Club.

"So when does *she* get home?" he says. "Tomorrow morning?"

He says it like it's a joke, but before anybody can laugh, I look him in the eye and say, "Shut your mouth, Dwyer!"

"Hey!" he says, like I've got him all wrong. "I'm just kidding. Can't you take a joke?"

I'm still looking him in the eye and I say, "In case nobody's ever told you before, Dwyer, let me be the first. You're an asshole!"

I don't wait for him to answer. I turn on my heels and I'm out of there. I can hear everybody behind me—laughing at Dwyer and hooting over what I said to him—but as I set out on the long walk home, I'm pissed.

I'm pissed at Dwyer for being such an asshole and at Marlene for going out with him and at Janice for playing up to him. I'm pissed at everybody! Including, I admit it, my mother, who, face it, isn't everything she should be.

But mostly, I'm pissed at God for making me part of a species that's half human and half male. I'm thinking we'd all be better off if we were sexless like amoebas.

That's what I'm thinking. It's ridiculous. I know that now. But at the time, I hadn't met Gary Everson.

Two

There's a garden behind the public library, but nobody seems to know about it but me. I noticed it out the back window of the library one day when I was doing research on the Cherokee Indians for my American History class.

Since the day I first noticed the garden, I've never seen anybody in it, although there must be a gardener who takes care of it because it's so well kept. But I've never seen him either.

So I think of it as my secret garden. And sometimes, when I have a lot on my mind, I just go there and try to chill myself out.

It's only a little garden, a patch of grass and flowers that looks out on nothing more beautiful than an alleyway and the back entrances to a bunch of stores. But it's amazing how well it works.

Except just now, as I walk up Elm Street, heading for home, I'm not thinking about my secret garden. I've got too much on my mind.

It isn't Dwyer that I'm thinking about. He's such a jerk that he isn't worth my time. It's what he said about my mother. What he implied. That she's, you know, sort of loose.

The thing is, I hate to admit it, even to myself, but I guess, in a way, it's probably true.

Not that I hold it against her. Exactly. My

9

mother's a really terrific person. And even though we don't exactly see eye to eye on everything, I really love her. And I'm not just saying that.

It's just that her life got all messed up and turned around when my father got killed in Vietnam right after I was born, in the last days of the war.

She probably should have left Waterford when it happened and made a new life for herself some-where. She was still young and pretty.

She still is. She's very pretty and she's very smart. And she's a good worker, too.

But I guess she couldn't tear herself away from the memories—of how it was before my father went off to Vietnam, when he was alive and the two of them were so much in love.

I guess she still can't—tear herself away from the memories, I mean.

And I guess, if that happened to me—if I was a really smart and good-looking young woman, who was left alone to bring up my kid in a town where all the eligible men were already married to friends of mine—I suppose I'd get so lonely after a while that I'd end up in a better-than-nothing relationship with somebody who wasn't all that eligible.

Like David Manion, who's married and has two kids in college and is the lawyer my mother works for.

He's also the one who got my mother the job at the country club.

And when my mother doesn't come home until the next morning, which hasn't happened for quite a while, it's usually because she's spent the night working late at the office, helping David Manion prepare for a big law case.

At least, that's what she says.

Only nobody believes her, including me. Especially since, for the last couple of years, David Manion seems to get most of his big law cases during the summer, after the country club's opened for the season and he's moved his wife out to their cottage at the lake.

So, how do I feel about that? About my mother and David Manion?

How do you think I feel?

Lousy. That's how I feel. And that's what I'm thinking about—about how lousy I feel—when I hear somebody crunching the pebbles in the driveway that cuts across the sidewalk right in front of me and leads around to the back of the public library and my secret garden.

Up until now, I hadn't even realized I was getting close to the library. In fact, I was so wrapped up in thinking about how lousy I feel, I probably would have walked right past it without even noticing it.

But now as I look up the driveway, I see somebody walking toward me, as if he's just come out from behind the library, as if he's been visiting my secret garden.

It's a pretty dark night with just a sliver of moon in the sky, but without even seeing his face, I recognize the guy who's walking toward me the minute that I see him. From the size of him and the way that he carries himself, like he owns the world, it's got to be Brian Avery.

Which is incredible. I mean, the idea of Brian Avery knowing about my secret garden and actually sharing it with me is beyond belief because Brian Avery is anything but a secret garden kind of guy.

Brian Avery is a tennis court kind of guy—a big, good-looking, super-rich superjock, who's got all the money in the world but hardly a brain in his head.

11

For example, he's a senior this year, the captain and the star of the tennis team, but last year, when he was just a junior and already the best player on the team, he missed out on a couple of our biggest matches because he couldn't keep up the passing average you need to be eligible. And believe me, keeping up a passing average at Waterford High is not that big a deal. I mean, you don't have to be a nuclear physicist or anything. In fact, you don't have to be much more than present.

But I guess Brian's done okay so far this year, or else I would have heard about him being declared ineligible in the school paper and around the halls.

But anyway, at about the same time that I spot Brian Avery, he spots me. And even though Brian hardly knows me and has never spoken a word to me before now, he calls to me.

"Angelica?"

I'm surprised that he even knows my name.

"Hi," I say, surprised.

"Great night!" he says, beaming. Then, looking up at the sky, he says, "Boy!"

Even though I don't happen to share his enthusiasm for the night, I nod and say, "Yeah."

"Where you coming from?" he says. "You need a lift? I've got my 'vette. I'll run you home. Is that where you're going? You live up on Academy, right? Come on. I'm over here."

And with that, he starts walking toward the curb where his bright red Corvette is parked and poised for takeoff.

"Work."

Brian stops and turns back to me.

"Huh?" he says.

"I'm coming from work," I tell him. "And I don't live on Academy Street. I live on Eastern

12

Boulevard. But I don't really need a lift because it's such a nice night that I feel like walking. But thanks anyway."

As if it couldn't matter less to him, Brian takes another look at the sky, shakes his head, and says, "Well, you've got a great night for it!"

"Yeah," I say.

"Well," he says, "take it easy!"

And with that, he turns and walks over to his 'vette and jumps in behind the wheel and, without checking to see if anything's coming, as if nothing would dare, he zooms off into the night.

For a moment I stand there, watching after him, thinking how strange life is and wondering if they could have torn out the garden behind the library and replaced it with an all-night tennis court.

I decide I'd better take a look. I head up the driveway.

As I walk, I don't crunch the pebbles in the two narrow tracks that make up the driveway. I walk on the grassy ridge between them. Not because I'm sneaking up on anybody or anything like that. But just because that's the way I always do it. It's quieter that way and more comfortable and the pebbles don't get into your shoes.

But if there *were* somebody back there in my secret garden, I could understand why he might *think* I was sneaking up on him.

Anyway, that's what Gary Everson seems to think.

When I turn the corner at the back of the library, I see Gary, standing there in my secret garden, with his back to me, fiddling with what turns out to be his wallet.

I'm surprised to see him, of course. I'm surprised

to see *anybody*. But my surprise is nothing compared to his.

When I say "Hi," just to let him know that I'm there, Gary practically jumps out of his skin. And the way he whips around and crouches down and stuffs his wallet in his back pocket, all at the same time, he looks like he's getting set to beat it out of there.

But when he sees that it's only me, as if he can't quite believe it, he says, "Angelica?"

Which makes him the second person in a row who knows my name when I didn't think he did.

"Sorry," I say. "I didn't mean to . . ."

"Oh." He smiles. "That's okay."

Easing up out of his crouch, he stuffs his hands in his pockets and, giving me this kind of half-curious half-amused look, he says, "How'd you know about this place?"

"The Cherokees," I tell him.

He laughs.

"I was doing a paper," I explain, "for American History, in the library."

"And you bumped into a Cherokee?" he says.

I laugh.

"A bunch of them," I tell him.

"They know all the best places," he says.

"Yeah," I say. "How about you?"

"Detectives," he says.

"Oh," I say, like I know what he's talking about.

"Dashiell Hammett," he says. "Ross Mac-Donald. Raymond Chandler. Elmore Leonard. Robert Parker. Ed McBain. You know them?"

"No."

"They write mysteries," he says. "I read them."

"In there?" I ask, nodding toward the library.

14

Gary nods and smiles.

"I hate TV," he says. "We don't even own one."

"What do you do?" I ask him. "Besides reading mysteries, I mean. Instead of watching TV, I mean."

Not too smooth, I admit. But the thing is, I can't believe I'm talking to this guy that I've never talked to before as if the two of us were a couple of old friends.

Gary Everson, I should probably tell you, is about the sexiest-looking guy you ever saw. He's really tall. Maybe six feet tall. And lean, but not skinny. And he's got these warm brown eyes. And this shy smile. And this mane of silky chestnut hair that hangs down almost to his shoulders and is the envy of every girl at school.

But the point is, I hardly know him. And not just because he's a big deal senior and I'm just a lowly junior, because hardly any of the seniors know him either.

Gary's new in town, since last summer, when he moved here from Scarsdale with his parents. And even though he could have fit right in with the college-bound clique that practically runs the senior class, I guess he didn't want to because, as smart and as funny as Gary's supposed to be, with his killer good looks and his laid-back charm, I'm sure they'd have loved to have him join up with them.

Although I suppose, if it came right down to it, everybody in that crowd would have wanted him to dress the same way that all of them do, which is kind of preppie, and Gary generally dresses kind of military surplus. Right now, for example, he's wearing a khaki-colored GI jacket and chinos and Nikes—which on him looks great.

15

"Besides reading mysteries?" he says. "I explore."

I look at him.

"There's a lot to see," he says.

"Here?" I ask him.

He smiles and nods.

"Here and there," he says. "What do you do?"

"Besides watching TV?" I ask him.

He smiles.

"Yes," he says.

"Read," I say. "Biographies, mostly."

He nods.

"So what kind of person *is* Vanna White?" he asks me.

He's so straight-faced, it takes me a second before I realize that he's teasing me.

I smile and say, "Ask me about Lillian Hellman."

"She lived with Dashiell Hammett," he says.

"That's not what she's famous for," I tell him.

He smiles.

"She wrote plays," he says.

"I read them too," I tell him. "Her plays and other peoples'. When I'm not reading biographies or watching TV, I mean. And I work."

"At the Olympic," he says.

I guess he must have seen me behind the candy counter, although I can't remember seeing him— which I would if I had.

"Is that where you're coming from?" he asks me.

I nod.

"Show business," I say. "It's my life."

He laughs.

"Who's that?"

I've noticed the headlights of a car, coming up

16

the alleyway that runs around to the back entrances of the stores behind the garden.

"Police," he says.

I don't know how he can tell from where we're standing, but as the headlights sweep over us and the car moves abreast of us, I see that he's right.

We both stand there watching the police car as it slows to a crawl opposite us and then picks up speed and continues on.

Then, turning to me, he says—Gary Everson, the sexiest-looking guy you ever saw says—"Where are you going now?"

"Home," I tell him.

"I'll walk you," he says. "Unless you'd rather . . ."

"No," I tell him.

I can't think of anything I'd rather.

"Great," he says.

Which is just what I was thinking.

Three

"Can you keep a secret?"

I've asked Gary about Brian Avery. Well, I didn't "ask him," exactly. What I said was, "I didn't know you hung around with Brian Avery," which is about the same thing as asking.

So now I tell him, "Sure, I can," although I'm a little puzzled about why Gary's hanging around with Brian Avery should be a secret, if that's the secret that Gary means for me to keep. But what else could it be?

Gary looks over at me. He looks into my eyes.

I feel my knees wobble under me. He's got such incredible eyes! They're penetrating, like searchlights, but at the same time they're warm, like candlelight.

He smiles at me.

It's such a friendly smile.

And then tells me the secret about him and Brian. He's tutoring him—Gary's tutoring Brian—and he has been all this semester, so Brian can keep his grades up and be eligible to play tennis.

I'm amazed. I mean, it's such an incredibly nice thing to do and so hard, considering how dense Brian's supposed to be. And I never suspected, not for a second, that Gary, being a newcomer to school and everything, would have that kind of school spirit.

He laughs at that.

"It isn't school spirit?" I ask him.

He shakes his head, which is a relief, I admit, because I never understood why people want to get all worked up about their school being better than somebody else's school, anyway.

Better at what? Playing football? Who cares?

Not me.

Not Gary either.

"He pays me," he says.

Yay, team!

"Oh," I say. "So why is it such a big secret?"

"Brian's embarrassed."

"Oh," I say. "Sure."

I guess I'd be embarrassed, too, if I needed somebody to help me through Health Sciences.

"He's not a bad guy," Gary says. "He's just a little . . ."

He shrugs.

"Spoiled?" I ask.

"Yeah," he says. "It's not easy being rich."

"I wouldn't know," I say.

Gary smiles.

"Me, neither," he says.

I don't know if he's kidding or not. I mean, I've always thought that Gary had lots of money, even if I've never actually seen him throwing it around like other kids with money do. He doesn't spend it on clothes, that's for sure.

But I know he lives in this beautiful model home that his father built as part of the Waterford Village Estates—which is this big real estate development that he's putting up out my way, on the edge of town. And I've seen him, sometimes, driving around in his father's BMW. So I've always figured that Gary had money, but he had better things to spend it on than clothes.

But maybe I was wrong. I mean, I suppose it's possible that Gary actually *needs* the money that he gets for tutoring Brian Avery.

"Don't you get an allowance?" I ask him.

Not that it's any of my business.

"No," he says.

Which is kind of surprising because even *I* get an allowance, although it isn't enough to live on.

"I could," he says. "I mean, I used to. When I was a kid."

"Years ago," I say.

Gary laughs.

"Until I was about twelve," he says.

"How old are you now?" I ask him.

"Seventeen," he says.

Perfect.

"You?" he asks.

"Sixteen," I tell him.

He smiles.

I don't know what it means, but I like it. Although, I admit, it makes me a little nervous. There's something about the way that Gary smiles. There's a kind of intimacy about it, like it's just between us two.

"So how come you don't?" I ask him. "Get an allowance, I mean. Still?"

Gary shrugs.

"I don't know," he says. "My father always says if you want to be your own man, you've got to pay your own way."

He laughs.

"What's your father always say?" he asks me.

20

"He's dead," I tell him.

"Oh," he says. "I'm sorry."

"Me too," I say. "I never knew him. He died in Vietnam. Right after I was born. But I look like him."

Gary nods and says, "He must have been a good-looking guy."

I think he's kidding.

He must be!

I look over at him, and he's smiling, but—

Oh, God! He isn't kidding!

What do I say?

"Oh, I don't know," I say.

I'm trying not to blush.

"He had really curly black hair that he couldn't do anything with, except keep it short. And a funny nose. And big cheekbones. And a hole in his chin."

Gary laughs.

"I like your dimple," he says.

I'm blushing. I'm not used to this.

"All three of them," he says.

I get dimples when I smile.

"So . . ." I say, searching for a way to switch the subject, because I'm afraid, if Gary says anything else about how he likes the way I look, I'll just melt into a puddle and disappear down a crack in the sidewalk. "You're your own man, huh?"

"Well." He laughs. "I *do* pay my own way."

"You mean you're *not* your own man?" I tease him.

Gary smiles and—like he really means it with all his heart—he says, "I'm trying."

I want to tell him, *That's good enough for me!* But I don't because I don't want Gary to think that I'm playing up to him, and I haven't got the nerve.

21

So, I just nod and smile, and we keep on walking.

We're still walking on Elm Street, but by now we're a long way from the library and downtown. Out here, Elm Street is really pretty with all of these huge old trees and old-fashioned street lamps lining the street on either side and all of these stately old houses set way back from the sidewalk.

Gary and I walk along in silence, moving from one pool of lamplight to the next, as if they were stepping-stones across a river of night.

There's nothing awkward about the silence, like there can be sometimes when you're walking along with somebody and neither of you has anything to say.

Both of us could probably find plenty of things to talk about if we wanted to. But I guess neither of us wants to, or needs to.

It's nice just walking along, listening to our footsteps and the wind in the trees and every now and then, a long way off, the barking of a dog and occasionally, the sound of a car—its low hum, rising and falling, as it approaches and passes us by and continues on.

I guess it's the cars that get me thinking about my father. I don't too often. But with the cars and Gary asking me about him and everything, after we've walked awhile, I find myself thinking about my father and, not too long after that, I hear myself saying, "He was an automobile mechanic."

Without missing a beat, as if he'd been listening in on my thoughts, Gary says, "Your father?"

I look at him.

"Yes," I tell him, "before he got drafted, he had his own garage on Arsenal Street. He was the best around. According to everybody. Foreign cars,

22

classic cars that they don't make parts for anymore. He made parts for them.

"He drove a tow truck, too. A wrecker. And fixed flats. And pumped gas. At least at first. Until he and his partner could afford to hire other people.

"He could have gone to college. He was smart enough, and he'd saved some money.

"And he probably could have gotten an athletic scholarship, even though he wasn't much taller than me. But he was solid. He got letters in three sports—baseball, football, and basketball. He was best at basketball.

"According to my mother, the guys he played with in high school used to call him 'Gunner' because of how many shots he took. But they didn't hold it against him because he made most of them. He was really good.

"But anyway, he didn't think of himself as a college type. He liked working with his hands. And he liked it here. In Waterford.

"So he started the garage with a friend of his, Ray Elliot. But Ray got bored with it, and after a while my father bought him out. But he kept the name—Elliot and Pierce, anyway. He said he liked the way it sounded.

"But my mother said he wanted to keep the door open in case Ray ever changed his mind and decided he wanted to come back.

"She helped him. My mother. She kept his books and did his correspondence and everything. She was so good at it that other people tried to hire her to work for them.

"David Manion, for one. That's who she works for now. As a legal secretary.

"But anyway, my father didn't want her to work.

And by then, they were making enough to live on without her having to work. So . . ."

"They had you," says Gary, completing my thought—*my life story!*—the way *I* should have, hours ago!

"God!" I say.

"What's wrong?" he says.

"I'm sorry," I tell him. "I don't do that. Ever. Even with my friends. I'm not a motor-mouth. Honestly. I just—"

"Felt like talking about your father," he says, "to me."

"Yeah," I say. "I guess."

"That's nice," he says. "Thanks."

"You don't mind?" I ask him. "Really?"

Gary shakes his head and says, "He sounds like he's somebody worth remembering."

"Yeah," I tell him. "I wish I did."

Gary nods and then after a second he says, "You want me to tell you about my father?"

I glance over at him to see if he's kidding.

He isn't. He's serious.

"If you feel like it," I tell him.

He laughs.

"There isn't that much to tell," he says. "Except for Waterford Village Estates. He's got his whole life wrapped up in that."

"It sounds fabulous," I tell him.

I've heard the commercials for it on the radio and seen the advertisements in the paper.

"Yeah," says Gary. "It's going to be. It's really taking off. About a year from now, Waterford's going to have one of the most beautiful planned communities in America."

He laughs. "I'm as bad as he is," he says. "My father, I mean. Spend enough time with me and,

24

before you know it, I'll pull out a brochure and try to sell you a house. But don't you live someplace around here?''

We've passed my house. *God!*

"Yes," I say. "Back there. The white one."

Gary smiles.

"Hard to miss," he says.

I feel myself starting to blush again.

"Yes," I tell him.

He takes my hand.

"I'll show you the way," he says.

I manage to say, "Thanks," but the way my heart's pounding, I'm not sure if he can hear me.

My mother's home. I can tell by the way the light is shining in her room on the second floor.

I tell myself I'm lucky that she isn't looking out of her window. I don't want her seeing me with Gary because I know she'll make a big deal out of it. She always does, whenever I go out with a boy, or even if she just sees me with one.

She tells me it's because she doesn't want me growing up too fast, but the way she acts, it's more like she doesn't want me growing up at all. It's something we fight about all the time.

But anyway, Gary walks me to my door—to the bottom of the steps that lead up to my door— holding my hand the whole time.

And I climb the first step and turn back to him, and he kisses me.

Yes! It happens so fast and feels so fabulous that I barely have time to feel amazed before I'm lost in the thrill of it.

And when I open my eyes and see Gary standing there, looking into my eyes and smiling at me, I'm so blown away that I tell him yes when he asks me, "Are you doing anything Saturday night?"

I say yes because I'm on the moon and, even though I can hardly believe it, I *think* Gary's asked me if I want to *go out* Saturday night, and the answer to that is definitely yes.

But when Gary says, "Oh," and looks disappointed, I fast rewind the tape in my head and play it back and hear his question the way that he asked it.

"I mean no!"

I almost shout it. "I'm *not* doing anything Saturday. Next Saturday, you mean?"

Gary smiles and nods.

"A week from tonight," he says.

"Nothing," I tell him, "except work. But I'm usually done by nine-fifteen."

"You want to do something?" he says.

"Anything you say," I tell him. Or my mouth does. But there it is. I break up. And blush. *I'm so embarrassed!*

And Gary breaks up too.

"I won't hold you to it," he says.

"Thanks," I say.

"This time anyway," he says.

"That's very kind of you," I tell him.

"I'm trying," he says.

"That's good enough for me," I tell him.

He smiles and says good night.

And kisses me again.

And then he lets go of my hand, and he's gone. *He's* gone? *God!* You should see *me!*

Four

As I come through the front door, I shout hello. I want to shout hallelujah!, but I don't because I'm I'm afraid my mother will think I've joined a cult and call in the brainwashers, and I don't want my brain scrubbed. Not now. I want to remember how good I'm feeling for the rest of my life.

I mean, I know it sounds corny, but I feel like Sleeping Beauty must have felt, right after she'd been kissed by Prince Charming. Exactly!

And Gary—*God!*—he's so incredible. To look at. And be with. And so sexy—*God!*—I *would* do anything he asked me to!

"Who was that, honey?"

My mother calls down the stairs to me.

Christ! I think. *She saw us!*

Hoping I'm wrong and doing my best to sound like innocence itself, I shout back up the stairs to her, "Who was who?"

She shouts down to me.

"That!" she says.

Which means that she saw us.

Great! I think.

"Oh," I say, trying to make it sound like it's no big deal, "just Gary."

And then—before she can shout, Gary who?—I

27

go charging up the stairs, shouting the first thing that pops into my head.

"You're home early," I shout.

Which would be fine, except it isn't true. Not lately, anyway.

Last year, especially on weekends, after the country club had opened for the season and David Manion had shipped his wife off to their cottage at the lake, there was no telling when my mother would drag herself in. But so far this year, at least since they opened the club a couple of weeks ago, she's been getting home right about this time.

So it isn't true that my mother's home early. It just happens to be the best thing I can come up with on the spur of the moment.

Which is why I'm not exactly surprised when I reach the top of the stairs and walk into my mother's room and see her sitting at her desk by the window and she says, "No, I'm not. It's almost twelve."

"Really?" I say, like I'm totally surprised. "That late?"

And quickly, before she can answer, I plop myself down on her bed and I say, "So, how was your night?"

"Gary who?" she says.

"Gary Everson," I tell her, like Gary's nobody special.

"You look great!" I say.

"Do I know him?" she asks.

"Probably not," I tell her. "Hey!" I say. "You should see the picture we're playing!"

"Is he related to Ray Everson?" she says.

"It's really interesting," I tell her.

"The Village Estates man?" she says.

I shrug.

"I guess so," I say. "That's where he lives."

"You've been to his house?" she asks me, like it would be a major scandal if I had.

"No! Of course not," I tell her, like it would be a major scandal if I had. "It's called *Blue Velvet.*"

"How well do you know him?" she asks me.

"Gary?" I ask her.

"Yes," she says, like she's losing patience with me.

"Very," I tell her.

"Oh?" she says. "Then why haven't I ever heard of him before?"

"What is this?!" I ask her.

It comes out sounding angry, but I can't help it. I *am* angry. I don't like being cross-examined.

My mother heaves a sigh and shakes her head.

"I'm sorry," she says. "I heard voices down below."

"God!"

I jump up from her bed. I'm really pissed now. If there's one thing I hate more than being cross-examined, it's being spied on.

"I didn't mean to spy," she says.

"I'll bet!" I tell her.

"I didn't," she insists.

"Look!" I tell her, "I don't know what you're thinking—"

"Nothing!" she says.

"Good!" I tell her. "Because Gary's really nice. And I like him. A lot."

"Apparently," she says.

"Mom!" I shout. "All I did was—"

"I know what you did," she says.

"So . . . ?" I say. "I didn't do anything wrong, did I?"

"Are you going to see him again?" she asks me.

29

"Yes," I tell her. "Next Saturday night. After work."

"I'll have to meet him before then."

"Mom!"

"Like always," she says.

"But, Mom . . ."

"Particularly since they're new in town," she says, "and nobody knows them."

"I know *him*," I tell her.

"But I've seen her," she says. "Mrs. Everson. Shopping at Milano's."

"So?" I ask her. "What's she like?"

"Very put together," she says.

"Like you," I tell her.

"I wish," she says.

"What do you mean?"

"I don't know," she says. "She looks like—like she just stepped out of a fashion magazine and brought her hair dresser along with her. You know what I mean?"

"You can't hate her because she's rich."

"I don't hate her at all," she says. "It's just that she's kind of glossy, that's all."

"So?"

"So I want to meet Gary before you go out with him," she says.

"Because his mother's glossy?" I ask her.

"Because *your* mother's choosy," she says, "about who her daughter goes out with."

"Which is why her daughter never goes out with anybody!" I tell her.

"Of course you do," she says. "Maybe some evening this week."

I tell myself not to say it, but out it comes.

"You mean, if you're not working late with David Manion."

30

My mother looks me straight in the eye and says, "I won't be."

I'm tempted to say, *Why not? Hasn't he moved his wife out to the lake yet?* But I don't want to get my head handed to me. So I just say, "Good night," and before I get myself in real trouble, I head for the door.

"Honey?" my mother calls to me.

As I hit the doorway, I turn back to her.

"Why don't you trust me?" I shout.

"I do," she says. "I just don't know him."

"*I* do!"

"Do you?"

"Yes!"

"Well," she says, "now we both will."

"Thrilling!" I mutter.

"What?" she says.

"Good night," I say.

"Good night," she says.

It was, I think, *until I ran into you!*

Five

"Come on, Angel, we'll be late."

I'm still in bed. My mother's standing at the door, already dressed and ready for church. It's Sunday morning around ten o'clock, and I have to be at work before one.

"I think I'll skip it today," I tell her.

"Come on," she says. "You know once you get yourself there, you're always glad you went."

Which is true. I do like going to church. Usually. But today . . .

"I think I'll sleep a little more," I tell my mother.

I was up all night, thinking about Gary. I was trying to figure out how I can get Gary to meet my mother before Saturday night without telling him that if he doesn't my mother won't let me go out with him, because I know if I have to tell Gary that I can't go out with him unless my mother's met him and approved of him first, he's going to think that I'm a baby, which—when it comes to boys—is exactly how my mother treats me. Like I'm a baby.

"Tired or lazy?" she asks me.

"Both," I tell her.

"Well . . ." she says.

I can see that she's disappointed.

32

"I haven't sinned," I assure her.

She smiles.

"Well, then," she says, "I guess it's all right."

"Thanks," I tell her.

"I have to run out to the club after services," she says. "Big dinner tonight. Fathers and sons."

"I'll see you tonight then," I tell her.

"I wish we had more time together," she says.

I can see that she's feeling guilty, so I shrug and remind her, "We're a two-career family."

She nods.

"And anyway," I tell her, "it's the quality of the time that counts. Not the quantity."

She smiles.

"I'm sorry about last night," she says. "I hope you understand."

"It's for my own good," I tell her.

"Don't you think it is?" she asks me.

"I don't know," I tell her.

"You don't?" she says.

"No," I tell her. "The way you're trying to keep me a baby—"

"I'm *not*," she insists.

"I'm not sure if it's for my own good," I tell her, "or for yours."

"Mine?" she says.

"But I'm sorry, too," I tell her, "about last night."

She heaves a sigh.

"Thanks," she says. "I needed that."

"You're welcome," I tell her.

She smiles and says, "I guess we're both doing the best we can, huh?"

I suppose it's true. But I'm still angry enough about her spying on me and her insisting on meeting Gary before I go out with him that I don't want to admit it right now. So all I say is, "You're going to be late."

"Oh!" she says.

She looks at her watch.

"Ten of," she says. "I'll see you tonight."

As she says it, she's already heading out the door and pounding down the stairs.

I call to her.

"I'm doing the best *I* can," I shout.

I hear my mother laugh as she hits the bottom of the stairs.

"I know you are," she shouts to me. "And I love you."

I shout, "I love you too," to her.

But as I do, I hear the sound of the door closing behind her. So I guess she doesn't hear me. Which I feel bad about because, even if she can be a terrible pain in the ass sometimes, my mother's very hard to hate.

Nonetheless, I spend most of the morning trying.

Six

It's the sound of the car backing out of the driveway that gets me started.

Why that bugs me so much is because it's so typical. The car, I mean. The way my mother won't let me drive it, even though I've got a junior driver's license and she knows that I'm as good a driver as she is.

According to my mother, the reason she won't let me drive the car—which happens to be a classic '65 Ford Mustang in mint condition—is because it was my father's pride and joy, and she'd never forgive herself if anything happened to it.

Which doesn't make any sense, because my mother's got to know that the drunken driver who's waiting out there, just itching to sideswipe the first classic car that he sees, is just as likely to plow into her as he is into me.

So, I ask myself, *Seriously, why won't my mother let me drive the car? Really why?*

And the answer's pretty obvious. It's because, as close as we are and as close as we've always been, when it comes to boys, my mother doesn't trust me!

I mean, even though she treats me like I'm a baby, she also treats me like if I were out of her sight for five minutes—which I would be a lot more often if she'd let me use the car—I'd turn into a raving slut!

Honestly!

That's why on nights when I go out—whether it's with a boy or a bunch of kids or even with just my girlfriends—I have to get home hours before everybody else does. And that's why she got so uptight when she saw me and Gary kissing. And why she has to meet any boy who wants to go out with me. So she can make sure they're not any threat to my priceless virginity.

Can you imagine? In this day and age? I mean, you'd think she'd be worried because I *am* a virgin. You'd think she'd be concerned about my being backward or gay or something.

I mean, nobody's a virgin anymore! Except for me and Marlene. And I haven't talked to Marlene yet, today.

Although, if she let Dwyer—ugh!—I don't even want to think about it!

But the point is, everybody's done it!

Janice, Gayle, even Toby—if you happen to believe the story that she tells, the one that was supposed to be a deep dark secret, except that she told it to everybody in the English-speaking world, about her and this gonzo twenty-year-old counselor who she met at camp last summer.

Everybody!

I mean, except for Marlene—who happens to be a very religious Catholic—I'm about the only girl I know who's still holding out for Mr. Right.

Everybody else I know gave in to Mr. Now a long time ago.

So why haven't I?

Well, it isn't because I haven't had the chance. I have.

I mean, some of the guys who passed my mother's inspections turned out to be exactly the kind of guys she's afraid of—all hands and no patience.

I mean, face it, these days you don't have to be a Hollywood movie star for some horny guy to swear that he loves you and that he'd do absolutely anything for you, if only you'd do this one little thing for him.

Actually, about all you have to be is a girl, which I am.

So it's not surprising that I've had my chances—to become a woman, as they say. And it isn't like I haven't been tempted. Or like there haven't been times when I've told myself, *As long as you've gone this far, what the hell, you might as well!* And times when I wound up feeling awful about letting some boy think that I would, long after I'd already decided that I wouldn't.

I mean, even though I'm a virgin, I'm not exactly Snow White. But I'm not exactly Alexis Carrington either.

I'm just me. Whoever that is.

But you'd think, whoever I am, my mother would trust me a little when it came to boys—and cars.

I mean, except for boys—and cars—she's trusted me a lot with almost everything else for as long as I can remember.

I mean, she practically had to, since, on the day she lost my father over sixteen years ago—because she'd already lost both of her parents before then—my mother's whole world suddenly boiled down to just her and me.

Which is why, from the very beginning, my mother and I were like a team. We always shared everything—the games we played, the food we ate and, until I was old enough to face the bogeyman on my own, even the bed we slept in.

We went shopping together for groceries and clothes and hardware. We went to the movies together and took little trips together. When one of us had to go to the doctor, we both went. And when, at the end of the month, we didn't have enough money to pay both the oil bill and the telephone bill, which happened more then once, we took turns making excuses to the one who wound up with the bounced check.

In fact, when I think about it, about the only thing we didn't share as I was growing up is, we never talked about the men in my mother's life. They were my mother's business. But the men in my life—the boys—they were my mother's business too.

We always talked about them—from the time I first noticed that there were boys right up until the time that my mother decided I was old enough to go out with them, which wasn't until last June when I turned sixteen.

Except even if I was old enough to go out with boys, my mother told me, I wasn't experienced enough to figure out which boys I should go out with.

Which was why, she told me, she'd have to meet any boy I wanted to go out with before I went out with him.

I might think she was being "overprotective," she said, if such a thing was possible in today's world, but the truth was, she was only being "responsible."

I told her that what she was being was "unfair."

"I'm sorry you don't understand," she told me,

38

"but someday you will, and you'll thank me for looking out for you."

Well, that day has yet to come.

And as I lie here in my bed, listening to the sound of my father's classic '65 Ford Mustang, purring off into the distance, I am not grateful. What I am is upset. And why I'm upset is that I've got a Major Problem.

There's this guy, Gary, who I really like, but I don't know if he really likes me, and I'm afraid if he finds out that he has to pass my mother's inspection before I can go out with him, he'll suddenly realize that I'm just a kid and not exactly the catch of the century either, and he'll just write me off as some girl that he happened to kiss once—*or was it twice?*—one warm spring night, a long time ago.

Which means that all I've got to do now is figure out how to get Gary inspected without giving him a chance to figure out that he's being inspected, or else I've got to lie to my mother and tell her that I've broken my date with Gary and then go out with him behind her back.

But those are my choices, and that's the decision I'll have to make—just as soon as I wake up.

As if I could get back to sleep now. Damn it! Why does life have to be so complicated!

Seven

"You want to come in?"

"Sure."

"My mother's home."

Gary smiles.

"Does she bite?" he asks.

"No," I tell him.

"So?" he says.

It's that night, Sunday night, and we're standing at my front door. Although it was the last thing in the world I expected, when I finished work about half an hour ago Gary was standing underneath the marquee outside the theatre.

At first, I didn't know if he was waiting for me or just getting out of the rain. It was pouring out—coming down so hard that the raindrops were bouncing off the street and dancing on the tops of cars.

Gary was soaking wet, but from the smile on his face, I could see that he was enjoying it. In fact, he was so caught up in watching the downpour, he didn't even notice me coming out of the theatre and walking up behind him.

I said, "Hello."

And when he turned to me, grinning like a kid at an amusement park—with his hair all wet and the rain streaming down his face—he looked so incredibly fresh, so happy and so alive, it was all I could do to stop myself from throwing my arms around him and kissing him right then and there.

But somehow I managed to restrain myself.

"What brings you here?" I asked him.

"I thought I might walk you home," he said.

I was thrilled and sure that he could see it, so I looked out at the rain and said, "What made you think that?"

He smiled and told me, "It was a nice night up until about five minutes ago."

"It must have seen me coming," I told him.

He laughed at that.

And because Gary's laugh is so infectious, I laughed too. And then we went on like that for a couple of minutes—standing under the marquee, joking around and talking about nothing in particular—while we waited for the rain to let up and studied each other's eyes.

But then, after a while, Gary spotted a bus coming up the street, and he looked at me, and I looked at him, and without either of us saying a word, he took my hand and we took off, running for the corner and the bus stop.

I got soaked, of course. But I didn't care because Gary was just as soaked as I was. In fact, when we got on the bus, Gary asked the bus driver if this was the bus to the Wet T-shirt Contest. Which was pretty funny—even the bus driver laughed—but it also made me look down at my blouse to see if anything was showing.

As usual, nothing was. I mean, I own a bra, but it's purely ceremonial.

I've got good legs, though. A little chunky in the thighs and butt, maybe, but nicely shaped. I look

41

good in jeans, even wet jeans, which I happened to be wearing.

But anyway, Gary and I took a seat on the bus and we made a bargain with the rain. We agreed, if neither of us mentioned the rain for as long as we were on the bus, by the time we got off the bus, the rain would stop.

As you can imagine, with both of us sitting there soaked, and the rain pelting against the bus windows, and the windshield wipers scraping and slamming away, it was a hard bargain to keep.

Right off the bat, thinking that I'd take our minds off of what was happening all around us, I asked Gary, "What were you doing before it started—?" and almost blew it, right there. "I mean, before you decided to come and pick me up," I said.

And Gary laughed at my almost mentioning the unmentionable word. But then, he told me, he'd been hanging out at Dominick's, which is this kind of boys-only video arcade that used to be an old-fashioned, boys-only pool hall over on Washington Street.

I was kind of surprised. I mean, I've never been to Dominick's myself. I don't think any girl ever has—or would ever want to—because of how ratty it looks. At least from the sidewalk.

It looks real dark and smokey inside and, from what I've heard, besides the regular high school crowd there's a bunch of older guys who hang around there—guys who are out of work and need a shave and could use a shower and always have either a cigarette or a matchstick hanging out of their mouths.

So I asked Gary what he was doing there, figuring he'd tell me he was playing the video games.

But he said he didn't really like video games, that playing them reminded him too much of watching TV, which he doesn't like to do because it makes him feel like he's wasting his time.

No, he said, he spent his time at Dominick's, hanging around the pool tables that they still have in the back. He said he was trying to learn how to shoot pool—which he said was a game that required real skill and incredible concentration. He said he enjoyed the education that the old-timers were giving him, almost as much as they enjoyed his paying them for it.

"At a quarter a game," he said, "you can learn a lot for a dollar."

I thought it was odd, Gary's wanting to learn to play pool. But on the other hand, I thought it was interesting too. I mean, it's one of the things I like about Gary—that he's not like everybody else.

But anyway, what with talking about Dominick's and what a great game pool is and everything, we managed to get through the whole bus ride without either one of us ever mentioning the you-know-what.

Except the you-know-what didn't seem to notice, because when we got off the bus at my stop, which is two blocks away from my house, it was still coming down in buckets.

Not that it made any difference. I mean, the two of us were already so wet that we couldn't get much wetter.

So we decided to just ignore it. With the streets all to ourselves, we just strolled to my house, slow and easy, as if it were the middle of the day and the sun was shining.

Except Gary was holding my hand—which I guess he might not have done if it actually had been the middle of the day—and I was feeling like Fate was on my side.

I mean, with Gary showing up at the theatre the way he did and us only a couple of blocks from my house and soaking wet from the rain, what could be more natural than for me to invite him into the house to dry off?

And if he accepted my invitation—which I thought he would—and my mother happened to be home from work—which I thought she was—then what could be simpler than introducing them to each other?

"Mom?"

As I open the front door and step inside the house, I call to my mother to let her know that I'm home.

Gary steps through the door behind me. Standing there in the front hallway just inside the front door, he glances around at the living room, off to his left, and the dining room, off to his right.

I wonder what my house must look like to a guy who lives in a beautiful model home. Not so hot, I imagine.

Gary catches me watching him checking the place out.

"Nice," he says. "Dry."

I laugh.

"Mom?"

I call again, but still she doesn't answer.

Shit! I think. *She isn't home, yet!*

I look at Gary.

He smiles and says, "She probably got caught in the whatchamacallit."

"Yes," I say. But I'm thinking, *Oh, my God! We're alone!*

"Well," I say, trying my best to put the thought

44

out of my mind, "you might as well stay until it lets up a little."

"Might as well," he says.

I reach around him to close the door.

But as I do, he takes me in his arms, and he kisses me. And as he kisses me, he leans back against the door, so that, as the door closes, I fall against him.

And I feel his whole body, pressing hard against me. And I press my whole body, hard against his. And I feel his tongue on my lips. And I open my mouth to his tongue.

And then, just at that moment, I guess the rain stops, because suddenly, although I haven't heard it before, from upstairs, I hear the sound of the shower, running in the bathroom.

She's home!

I pull away from Gary.

"What's wrong?" he says.

"My mother's home," I tell him.

"She is?" he says.

I'm about to tell him, *Listen! Hear the shower? That's her!* but just then I hear my mother, upstairs, turning the shower off.

And Gary hears it too. And he smiles and shakes his head and says, "For a minute there, I thought, maybe, you didn't like . . ."

Meaning that he thought I didn't like him kissing me. Can you imagine?! I mean, I'm still half out of my head from it!

In fact, I can hardly keep my voice from quavering as I look into his eyes and shake my head and say, "No. I *did.*"

"That's a relief," he says.

And you should see the way he smiles. I mean,

45

it's such a great smile, it makes me want to get right back to doing what we were doing before.

But with my mother upstairs and Saturday night still up in the air, I realize this isn't the time or place. It's the time to clear my head and steady my heartbeat, and it's the place to take a deep breath and change the subject.

"Want me to get you a towel?"

Gary smiles.

"If it's not too much trouble," he says.

"No," I tell him. "I'll be right back."

But as I turn and look up the stairs that lead to the second floor, I see my mother, clumping down the stairs. She's drying her hair with a towel, so she doesn't see me.

But I see her, all right. Most of her. And so does Gary. Because she's wearing this emerald green robe that she always wears. Except until now, I never realized it was so short—it barely reaches her knees—and so loose at the top!

"Mom!"

She's about halfway down the stairs when she looks up and sees me and Gary and stops dead in her tracks.

"Oh!" she says.

"I didn't know . . ." she says.

"Excuse me," she says.

And she turns around and scurries back up the stairs and disappears out of sight.

The moment she's gone, I turn to Gary. He's still looking up the stairs. But now he turns to me—blushing a little but with this smile on his face—and he says, "Wow!"

I know exactly what he means. I'm thinking, *Why did I have to look like my father?*

But I nod my head and say, "Yeah, isn't she?"

"Should I go?" he asks.

"No," I say. "Why?"

"Because," he says. And then he laughs and he shrugs and he says, "I don't know."

"Hello."

She's back. That fast. My mother.

But now she's wearing her other robe, the floor-length black velour one with the scarlet belt around its gathered empire waist. And she's got her hair wrapped up in a white towel that's set like a turban high on her head. So that now, as my mother glides down the stairs, she looks like a visiting princess from some exotic land, impossibly tall and depressingly pretty.

As she arrives at the bottom of the stairs, she shoots me a look and, gliding right by me, she extends her hand to Gary, uncorks a dazzling smile, and says, "You must be Gary."

Jesus! I think. *What if he wasn't?*

"Yes," says Gary.

He takes her hand and, for a second, I think, *He's going to kiss it!*

But Gary's just shakes my mother's hand and returns her dazzling smile with an equally dazzling smile of his own and says, "How do you do?"

"This is my mother," I say.

Not that anybody's listening. I mean, the two of them are practically riveted to each other.

"A lot better," says my mother, "since I got out of the rain."

She releases Gary's hand and turns to me.

"Angelica?" she says. "Did you offer Gary a towel?"

"You want a towel?" I ask him.

"No," he says.

Which surprises me.

47

"Thanks," he says.

Then, turning back to my mother, he says, "I haven't got far to go."

"Would you like some coffee?" my mother asks him.

"No," says Gary. "Thank you."

"Tea?" she says.

It's like, all of a sudden, she's turned into a stewardess!

"No, really," says Gary, "I've got to be going. I'm dripping all over your rug."

And drooling all over the front of your shirt! I think.

My mother laughs.

"Don't worry about that," she says.

Don't worry? I think. *If it were me, she'd have a fit!*

"No, really," Gary says. "I should be going. My father's out of town on business, so my mother's home alone—probably just watching television and wondering what's keeping me."

"Oh," says my mother.

She looks disappointed. But I'm thinking, *Watching television?! But I thought you said . . .*

"Would you like to call her?" my mother asks.

"No," says Gary. "Thank you. But I don't think so. That might just alarm her. I'll be home in a couple of minutes."

"Well," says my mother, uncorking another of her dazzling smiles. "I'm glad I got a chance to meet you."

"Me, too," says Gary, uncorking another of *his* dazzling smiles.

"Me, too," I say, just in case they've forgotten that I'm still there.

"I hope I see you again," says my mother.

"Me, too," says Gary.

And then he stands, smiling and following my mother with his eyes as she sweeps out of the front hallway, glides through the dining room, and disappears into the kitchen.

And then, as if my mother's disappearance was his cue to leave, he turns to me and says, "Well . . ."

"I'll get the door for you," I tell him.

"That's okay," he says.

He reaches for the door, opens it, and steps outside.

I go to the door to say good night.

Gary looks up at the sky.

"It's stopped raining," he says.

I look up at the sky.

"Yes," I agree.

He looks at me.

"She's very pretty," he says.

I look at him.

"The sky is blue," I tell him.

He laughs.

"What's hard to imagine," he says, "is how your father could have been even better looking than her."

"Huh?"

I can't believe my ears! Is Gary actually telling me that he thinks I'm better looking than my mother?

"Lucky you," he says.

He is! And from the way he's looking at me, he isn't kidding. He means it!

I don't know what to say. I think I say, *Lucky me*, but I'm not sure because, the next thing I know, Gary's kissing me.

Again. But not like before.

This time his kiss is sweet and tender.

But it's just as good as before. Maybe even better. I can't say, really.

All I know for sure is, after it's over, Gary says, "Good night," and then he turns and goes down the steps and down the front walk.

And when he reaches the sidewalk, he looks back at me and calls, "See you tomorrow."

And I think I say, *See you tomorrow*, back to him, but I'm not sure about that either.

What I'm sure of is, I stand there at the door, watching him move off down the street, until he disappears into the darkness and I can't see him anymore.

And then I close the door and I turn and I walk across the front hallway to the stairs and I climb them. And when I reach the second floor, I grab a towel out of the bathroom. And as I walk down the hall to my room, I dry my hair. And as I walk into my room and slip out of my clothes and let them drop where they fall, I dry the rest of me.

And as I drop the towel on the floor, I climb into bed. And as I pull the covers over me, I close my eyes.

And then, all of a sudden, from out of nowhere, it suddenly occurs to me that I never asked Gary about his TV. I never asked him why he told my mother that his mother was home watching TV, when he'd told me, just last night, that he didn't own a TV.

I wonder, could they have bought a TV between yesterday and today? Could they have suddenly decided that they were missing out on a good thing? Could they have developed a sudden craving for Phil Donahue? Or Oprah Winfrey?

And speaking of sudden cravings, what am I

50

doing, lying here, worrying about Gary's TV, when I could be fast asleep and dreaming about Gary?

Mmm . . . God! When he kissed me! When we first came in and I was reaching to close the door!

God! It's a good thing my mother was home. God! But imagine if she wasn't!

Mmm .

Eight

"Asleep?"

"Huh?"

Startled by the sound of my mother's voice, I open my eyes—I must have dozed off for a second—and see her standing in the doorway.

"No," I lie.

God! I think, *I forgot all about her!*

"Well," I say, "has the jury reached a verdict?" She laughs.

"Well," she says, "he seems nice . . ."

But the way she says it, it doesn't sound like she's all that impressed.

"And he's certainly attractive . . ." she says.

Attractive? I think. *If Gary's attractive, then who's great-looking?*

"And he isn't glossy," she admits.

"So?" I ask her, "I can go out with him?"

"But," she says, "he does seem awfully smooth, doesn't he?"

"Smooth?" I ask her.

"You know," she says, "charming."

"So?" I ask her. "Is there something wrong with that?"

"You don't think he works at it?" she asks me. "Just a little bit? At being charming?"

"No," I tell her. "I don't."

She heaves a sigh, and then she smiles at me and says, "Twelve o'clock."

Meaning it's okay for me to go out with Gary, which is terrific, but I have to be home by twelve o'clock, which is the pits.

"I'm not done with work until nine-fifteen!" I tell her.

"What are you going to do?" she asks me.

"I don't know," I tell her.

"Well," she says, "two hours and forty-five minutes ought to be long enough to do it. Don't you think?"

"No!" I tell her. "Not on a Saturday night!"

"It's been Saturday night before," she reminds me.

"But I never went out with a senior before!" I remind her.

"All the more reason," she says.

"Mom!" I say. I'm pleading with her.

"Angelica . . ." she says. She isn't buying it.

"But Mom . . . !" I say. I'm practically begging.

"Twelve," she says. She's not budging an inch.

"Thanks a lot," I say, sarcastically.

"Good night," she says, evenly.

"Yeah," I say, bitterly. "You, too."

She turns and switches off my light and closes my door.

And I lie there in the darkness, thinking how lousy it is that I have to be home by twelve and wondering why my mother has her heart set on winning the prize for raising the most backward girl in the world.

But after a second, I find myself thinking, *On the other hand, what could Gary and I do in three hours and forty-five minutes that we can't do in two hours and forty-five minutes?*

I laugh as I think of the answer—

An hour more of whatever we're doing.

And as I lie there in the darkness, imagining what that might be, I smile.

Nine

Beep-a-beep!

I'm standing at the kitchen counter, swilling orange juice and downing a fistful of vitamins when I hear Marlene out in front of my house honking for me.

It's the next morning, Monday morning, and I'm feeling about as happy as I've ever felt in my life.

I mean, I'm not exactly looking forward to telling Gary if he doesn't get me home by twelve o'clock Saturday night, I'll turn into a pumpkin. But as I grab my books and head for the front door, I tell myself that isn't the point.

The point is, whatever time Gary has to get me home, I'm going out with him.

This Saturday night, I tell myself, *I'm going out with Gary Everson. Me! Angelica Pierce!*

I can hardly believe it. And I can't wait to tell Marlene.

Except, as I come out the door and head for her car, I can see that she's not alone. She's got somebody with her, which she doesn't usually.

Usually, when Marlene comes to pick me up, like she does almost every morning when she doesn't have to go to the doctor for her allergy shots, she's alone. But not today.

Today, she's got somebody with her and the

somebody she's got with her—sitting in the front seat, beside her—is Toby.

And even though I'm just aching to tell Marlene about Gary and me, with Toby around, I'm not about to say a word, because maybe Marlene can keep a secret, but—face it—anything that Toby hears, the whole world knows, and I don't want to go through the week with everybody at school kidding me about Gary and asking me a lot of stupid questions like how did you meet him and what's he like and everything.

And if, for some reason, things don't work out between Gary and me on Saturday night—if something I do or say suddenly makes Gary realize that he's made a terrible mistake asking me out and he never asks me out again—then I don't want to go through the rest of my life with everybody in the world talking about how I blew it.

So, even though I'm dying to see the look on Marlene's face when I tell her about Gary and me, I don't say a word about it. Instead, as soon as I get into the car and we take off for school, I ask Marlene how things went at her house Saturday night.

Right away, Toby shoots me a look, like I shouldn't have brought up the subject, and then she rolls her eyes, like something incredible happened.

But if it did, whatever it was, Marlene doesn't seem to know about it because all she says is, "It was great!" and then, as if I needed convincing, she rattles on about how funny Dwyer was, how he'd seen the Robin Williams show the first time it was on, how he'd practically memorized it, how he knew the punch lines to all the jokes and sketches and everything and how he called out every one of them, every time, just a split second before Robin Williams got a chance to.

Which doesn't sound like a lot of fun to me. But then, I'm not in love with Dwyer and Marlene is.

So I say, "It sounds terrific!"

"Tell her about Janice," Toby says.

She shoots me another look.

"Oh," says Marlene, like it's no big deal. "Janice got sick. Dwyer brought over a case of beer. I don't know where he got it. It was warm."

"It was probably hot," says Toby.

Meaning it was stolen. But Marlene doesn't get it. She just goes on.

"Anyway," she says, "you know how Janice gets when she drinks."

"Sick," I say.

Janice is famous for vomiting whenever she drinks. It doesn't matter what it is or how little of it she drinks. She just can't hold it down.

"Yes," says Marlene. "But even worse than usual."

"Ick," I say.

"But Dwyer was so nice," she says.

Dwyer? I think. *Nice?*

"He drove her home," says Toby.

And she shoots me that look again.

Not that she has to. I know Dwyer. And I know Janice.

"Oh?" I say.

I try to keep the suspicion out of my voice, so Marlene won't hear it.

"He *can* be nice," Marlene says.

"I know," I say, although I actually don't. "But what about Janice?"

I'm sorry the second that I say it. But there it is.

"What do you mean?" says Marlene.

"She means Janice is a slut," says Toby.

Marlene looks at her and breaks out laughing.

"Janice and Dwyer?" she says.

"Janice and anybody!" says Toby.

"Dwyer hates Janice," says Marlene.

"How do you know?" I ask her.

"Because he's told me," she says. "Lots of times."

As Toby shoots me yet another look, I say, "Oh," like that settles it, but I'm thinking, *Oh-oh!!*

Ten

When we get to school, after Toby's peeled off for her homeroom, I tell Marlene that I've got something to tell her, and I ask her to meet me out at the baseball field for lunch.

The way it works at Waterford High School, you don't have to eat lunch in the cafeteria. You can eat anywhere you want to, in school or out, as long as you get back from lunch in time for your afternoon classes.

Usually, the gang I hang out with eats in the cafeteria, but sometimes we go across the street to the mall for a fast food feed.

We almost never go to the baseball field out behind the school, which is where a lot of the jocks and their girls hang out at lunchtime. That's why I want Marlene to meet me there—because I don't want anybody that I know around when I tell her about Gary and me.

"What is it?" Marlene asks me.

But the class bell is already ringing, and we're supposed to be in our homeroom seats before it stops.

"Later," I tell her.

And I take off, running for my homeroom.

Eleven

I see Gary between second and third periods. I've been looking forward to seeing him ever since last night.

I've imagined the way we meet in slow motion with romantic music playing under it. I've seen us loping down the corridor toward each other, meeting in a swirling embrace, kissing and swooning to the floor together. I've seen the floor turning into sand and the corridor turning into a beach and the pounding surf rushing up the beach and sweeping around us as we make love in the blazing, tropical sunlight.

But that isn't the way it actually goes.

The way it actually goes is, when I come out of my Spanish class and I'm walking up the corridor with Gayle, I see Gary going around a bend at the other end of the corridor, but he doesn't see me.

That's the way it actually goes.

And I don't see Gary again before lunch. And I don't see him at lunch either, because he isn't part of the beef-and-buns crowd that hangs around the bleachers out by the baseball field.

But I am. At least today.

And so is Marlene.

"Who is it?" she asks me.

This is after we've found ourselves a quiet spot in the corner of the bleachers, and I've told her that

I've met this incredible guy, and I'm going out with him Saturday night.

"Or do I have to guess?" she asks me.

"You'd never guess," I tell her. "He's a senior."

"That narrows it down," she says.

"You can't tell anybody," I tell her.

"Okay," she says. "So who?"

"I mean it," I tell her.

"So do I," she says.

"Okay," I say. "Gary Everson."

"Gary Everson?" she shouts.

I swear, she shouts it!

"Marlene!"

I look around at the jocks and their girls to see if anybody's listening. But they're much too wrapped up in themselves and one another to care about ordinary mortals like Marlene and me.

"Jesus!" I tell Marlene. "If I wanted everybody in the world to know, I would have taken an ad on TV!"

"I'm sorry," she says. "I'm just surprised."

"You're surprised!" I tell her.

"He's the new guy, right?" she says.

"Yeah," I tell her.

"Real cute, right?"

"Cute?" I ask her. "Is Rob Lowe cute?"

"He *isn't* Rob Lowe," she says.

"I'm not Cybil Shepherd," I tell her.

She looks at me like I'm crazy.

"They don't go out," she says.

"I *know,*" I tell her.

"Isn't he a Jew?" she says.

"Rob Lowe?" I ask her.

"Gary Everson," she says.

"Oh," I say. "I don't think so."

61

"He's from New York City, right?"

"Scarsdale," I tell her.

"That's in New York City," she says. "Isn't it?"

"I don't know," I say. "But everybody from New York City isn't a—isn't Jewish."

"According to my father, they are," she says.

"So what?" I ask her. "I mean, what if he is?"

She shrugs.

"Nothing," she says. "It's just . . . Isn't he into computers or something?"

"I don't think so," I tell her. "But he could be. I just met him."

"I don't know," she says.

"What?"

"Aren't they supposed to be pretty fast?"

"Who?"

"New York City people," she says.

"Oh," I say. "I don't know."

For a second, I remember Gary kissing me, his body pressing against mine, his tongue . . .

"Yes, you do," says Marlene.

I guess I'm blushing.

"I don't!" I insist.

"Come on!" she says. "How far did you go?"

I *am* blushing.

"I just let him kiss me good night," I tell her.

"And . . . ?" she says.

"And wished he'd never stop," I admit.

Marlene laughs.

"See what I mean?" she says.

"No!" I tell her.

"Yes, you do," she says.

I laugh.

"Yeah," I say. "But it's not because *he's* fast."

"Oh?" she says.

"It's because *I* am."

Marlene laughs at that, and so do I, until Marlene says, "Me, too."

And then I think about her and Dwyer.

"But you haven't . . . ?" I ask her. "Have you?"

"Me?" she says.

Like she'd never.

"Anyway," she says, "it's *you* we're talking about."

"Oh, yeah," I say, as if I'd forgotten.

"You wouldn't . . . ?" she says. "Would you?"

"Me?" I say.

Like I'd never.

Marlene smiles at me.

"Us virgins have to stick together," she says.

I smile back at her.

"Yeah," I say, "to the death."

"Well," she says, "let's not go overboard."

Which cracks me up.

"Okay," I say. "Just until we get married then. Or engaged. Or live with somebody."

Marlene takes a second to think it over.

"Well," she concedes, "until Saturday night, anyway."

I break up.

"You can count on me," I tell her.

Marlene heaves a sigh.

"Can I count on you?" I ask her.

Marlene heaves another sigh, and then she says, "What do you think about Janice?"

"You mean her and Dwyer?"

"Yeah," she says. "You don't think she'd . . . ?"

"Yes," I tell her. "I do."

Marlene nods her head.

"So do I," she says.

She looks me in the eye.

"But what about him?" she asks me. "You don't think he'd . . . ?"

Marlene knows what I think of Dwyer—how little I think of him—but because she's my best friend, I've never told her in so many words.

I don't tell her now either, although I'm tempted to, for her sake. I hate the idea of an idiot like Dwyer making a chump of her.

But since I've only got Toby's suspicions about Dwyer and Janice to go on, and I don't really know anything for sure, I keep my doubts to myself and answer her with a shrug.

And Marlene nods and heaves a sigh and says, "I hope you're wrong."

"I hope so too," I tell her.

Marlene heaves a sigh—a humongous one—and shakes her head.

For a second, neither of us says anything. But then, after a second, Marlene looks over at me and says, "So, you're going out with Gary Everson, huh?"

"Yeah," I say.

"His car or yours?" she asks me.

"Funny," I tell her.

"He *is* cute," she says.

"Yeah," I say. "But not a word, okay?"

Marlene smiles and draws her fingers across her lips, as if she was zipping them shut.

I smile back at her.

It doesn't hit me until later, how easily zippers come undone. I should have demanded staples.

Twelve

At the end of the day, I'm standing in front of my locker, trying to decide which books to lug home with me and which books to leave behind.

I haven't seen Gary again since I caught that glimpse of him this morning, but I've been thinking about him all day, and I'm thinking about him now.

I'm not paying any attention to Toby, who's standing beside me, sorting through the junk in her locker.

But now Toby says, "Are you doing anything Saturday night?"

She says it casually, as if she were just wondering. But when I look over at her, I can see that she's got just the hint of a grin playing around the corners of her mouth.

Does she know? I wonder. *Did Marlene tell her?*

"I don't know," I tell her.

Toby smiles.

"Oh," she says. "Because I was thinking about having everybody over to my house."

"Oh, yeah?" I say.

"Yeah," she says. "Because my mother and father are going to Rochester for the weekend, and I'm not supposed to have anybody over."

"Makes sense to me," I tell her.

"Except," she says, "if you're *going out* or something . . ."

She looks at me, like she's waiting for me to say something.

"What are you smiling about?" I ask her.

"Huh?" she says.

"Do you know something that I don't know?" I ask her.

"No!" she says, and she gives me this innocent look, like she can't imagine what I'm talking about.

"Because I don't know what I'm doing yet," I tell her.

"Oh," she says. "Well, if you're *not* going out . . ."

"Will you *still* be having everybody over?" I ask her.

For a second, Toby just looks at me.

It's like she wants to say no, but she knows, if she does it will be like admitting that she never planned on having everybody over to her house in the first place, like the whole thing was just a trick to get me to say, Gee, Toby, I'm sorry. I'd love to come to your house, Saturday night, but I can't, because, unfortunately, I've already made plans to go out with Gary Everson. *Which, of course, Toby already knows, but she can't let on that she knows because Marlene told her!*

Which is why, after she thinks it over for a second, she tilts her head and looks at me like I've asked her a really silly question and says, "Yes! Of course, I will."

"Great!" I say.

But now it's my turn to smile because now, unless Toby wants me to think she's a total liar, she'll *have to* invite everybody over to her house Saturday night, whether she wants to or not.

"Can I let you know?" I ask her. "If I can make it?"

"Sure," she says.

"Great!" I tell her.

And with that, I slam my locker shut and take off down the hall.

And I'm not smiling anymore because I'm really *pissed* at Marlene. I mean, she's supposed to be my *best friend*. I mean, even if my going out with Gary Everson is pretty hot news, you'd think she could have kept her mouth shut about it for at least *one day*.

But *nooo!* She had to go and *blab!* To *Toby*, of all people—*The Voice of America!*

"Hi, Angelica!"

"Hi."

The thing that gets me—*Gary!*

I'm just about to go out the door that leads out to the parking lot, when I realize that I just passed Gary coming in *and I hardly even noticed him!*

Amazed—and mortified—I whip around and there he is, standing right in front of me, looking into my eyes and grinning at me.

"Hi," I say.

Gary's grin blossoms into a smile.

"Do you know Wayne?" he says.

He looks over at this guy who's standing just behind him, Wayne Shuster.

Wayne's this weird-looking mathematical genius who stands about six-foot-twelve and weighs about a hundred pounds, soaking wet. But as weird as he looks, with everybody pushing by us and heading out the door and Gary standing so close to me and looking as if he might kiss me any second, I didn't even notice Wayne standing there.

"No," I tell Gary. "I mean, yes"—meaning I've

never been formally introduced to Wayne, but I know who he is—and I look over at Wayne and I say, "Hi."

Wayne blushes and drops his eyes to the floor and says, "Hello."

"Wayne and I are tutoring each other," Gary tells me. "I'm teaching him how to use a computer, and he's teaching me how to meet beautiful girls. Right, Wayne?"

Wayne chuckles.

"Yeah," he says. "But I have to go now."

"I'll catch up with you later," says Gary. "Okay?"

"Okay," says Wayne, and he glances over at me and says, "I'm pleased to have met you."

"Thank you," I tell him, but he's already turning away and slipping off into the crowd.

"He's cute," I tell Gary.

"You better watch out for him," says Gary. "He's hell on pretty girls."

I laugh.

"I better watch out for you," I tell him. "You're smooth."

He grins, like I've paid him a compliment.

"You think so?" he says.

"Not really," I tell him. "But my mother does."

"Is that good?" he asks me.

"Good enough," I tell him. "Oh!"

I've just remembered.

"What?" he says.

I shake my head.

"Nothing," I tell him.

Gary smiles.

"Come on," he says. "What is it?"

"Well," I say, "it's just your TV . . ."

"My TV?"

"You said you didn't own one," I remind him.

"Yeah . . . ?"

"But you told my mother—"

Gary laughs.

"You're a good listener," he says.

"When I'm interested," I tell him.

He smiles.

"That's nice," he says.

"So?" I say.

"So . . ." he says. He's still smiling, but now he looks embarrassed. "You're right," he says. "I don't own a TV."

I look at him.

"So," he says, "my mother wasn't home watching TV last night, like I said."

I don't say anything.

"So," he says, "you want to know why I told your mother that she was."

"Yeah," I say, "that was the question."

Gary shrugs, like he's not really sure.

"I guess I just didn't want to explain to your mother where my mother actually was," he says.

I nod and say, "Which was where?"

"In New York," he says. "Just for the weekend. To shop and see her friends. She's been kind of lonely."

"Oh," I say.

"But with my father out of town, I didn't want your mother to think my parents were the kind of people who'd just go off and . . ."

"Leave you stranded?" I say.

"Yes," he says. "They're not like that."

"You're seventeen," I remind him.

"I know," he says. "But sometimes, in a town as small as this, people have funny ideas about how other people should raise their children."

"So you just . . . ?"

Gary nods and looks down at the floor and—like a little boy confessing that he forgot to feed the cat—he says, "Lied."

He looks so adorable, I don't know whether I should spank him or give him an Oreo cookie and a glass of milk.

"You mean you 'smoothed it over,' " I tell him.

"Yes," he says, and he looks up from the floor and looks me in the eye and—smiling just a little—he says, "Do you forgive me?"

Silly question.

I mean, the way Gary's looking at me, if he'd just run over my dog—not that I own a dog—but if I did and he had, I'd probably forgive him in a second.

I mean, how am I supposed to hold a grudge against anybody who looks at me like that?

So I say, "What is there to forgive? I mean, it was a white lie, wasn't it? To protect your parents' reputation?"

"Yes," he says. "But—"

"So where's the harm?" I ask him.

Gary doesn't say anything. He just looks at me and grins. And then, after a second, he says, "So where are you going now?"

"Excuse me," somebody says—a big guy, a football player, Brooks, his name is—and without breaking stride, he plows right through us and heads out the door.

"Just home," I tell Gary.

I want to say, *Unless you've got a better idea,* but I manage to restrain myself.

"I've got a pile of homework," I tell him. "And there's a movie I want to see on TV tonight, so . . ."

I shrug.

A long moment passes with the two of us just looking into each other's eyes and neither one of us saying anything.

And then, because the way that Gary's looking at me is more than I can take, I say, "Where are you going?"

"Sorry," says another guy, and *he* squeezes between us and heads out the door.

Gary smiles.

"Just over here," he says and, taking my hand, he leads me out the door and over to the side of the building, out of the flow of traffic.

Leaning back against the side of the building, I look up at Gary and say, "Great idea!"

Still holding my hand, Gary smiles down at me and says, "Thanks."

"You're welcome," I tell him.

"I've been thinking about Saturday night," he says.

"Yeah?" I say, like I'm surprised.

Gary smiles.

"Have you?" he says.

"Oh," I say, "a little."

Gary grins.

"I think I can get the car," he says.

"Oh," I say. "Great!"

"So we can go anywhere," he says.

"Great!" I tell him.

"But I thought," he says, "if it's okay with you, I mean, we could go to Charlie's."

"Great!" I say.

I'm starting to sound like a broken record, I know, but the way Gary's smiling at me . . .

"You sure?" he says.

"No," I say. "I mean, yes. Charlie's would be . . ."

"Great?" he guesses.

I laugh.

"Fine," I tell him.

Gary laughs.

"It's pretty raunchy," he says.

"I've been there," I tell him. "I like it."

I have and I do. Charlie's—which is what everybody calls it, although it's actually named the Lakeside Inn—is this dumpy little place out at the lake. In the summer—which it's not yet—they have live music and dancing. They also serve pizza and steamers and beer. And the reason everybody goes there—aside from the lake and the music and the dancing and the pizza and the steamers—is they don't check IDs that often and, when they do, they don't usually look that close.

"Should I pick you up at the theatre?" he asks me.

God! I think. *This is really happening! I'm really going out with him!*

"Okay," I say.

"What time?" he says.

"Nine-fifteen," I say. "Or nine-thirty."

In case I want to change.

"Which?" he asks.

"Nine-thirty," I tell him.

Just in case.

"Great!" he says.

I laugh.

"It's contagious," he tells me.

And he looks into my eyes and squeezes my hand, and it suddenly occurs to me—standing there, leaning against the side of the building with Gary holding my hand and everybody streaming out the door—*There's no way I'm going to be able to keep this a secret!*

I mean, aside from seeing Gary every day at school—and being seen with him—when we show up at Charlie's Saturday night, everybody in town is going to know that we're going out.

And if something goes wrong and Gary never asks me out again, everybody in town is going to know that, too.

So, I realize, *since my going out with Gary was an impossible secret to keep anyway, I guess it was really pretty silly of me to ask Marlene to keep it.*

But still, I remind myself, *since I did ask her . . .*

"Hi, Angelica!"

And since she's supposed to be my best—Marlene!

"Hi, Gary!" she says.

Marlene and Toby and Gayle and Janice—the whole bunch of them—have just walked out the door together, and somebody must have spotted us because now they're all just standing there, gaping at us and grinning their heads off.

I try to pull my hand away from Gary's.

But Gary holds on tight, and he looks over at Marlene and the others, and he smiles at them like they're old friends of his, and he says, "Hi!"

I must look like a tomato, the way I'm blushing.

"You need a ride?" Marlene asks me.

She says it like she's being really friendly, but I'm still really pissed at her for blabbing my secret to Toby—and God knows who else—even if they would have found out about me and Gary sooner or later, anyway.

I tell myself I shouldn't even talk to her. But my good manners get the best of me.

"No," I say. "I don't."

73

Despite my good manners, it comes out pretty sharp. But Marlene doesn't seem to notice.

"Oh," she says, smiling like she's pleasantly surprised. "Okay. Bye!"

"Bye," I say.

"Bye, Gary," says Toby.

He says, "Good-bye."

And then they turn, Marlene and the rest of them, and as they head off into the parking lot, I swear, half of them are stifling giggles.

And Janice—God!—before she's taken two steps, I catch her looking back over her shoulder at Gary and me and, I swear, *she winks at me!*

Gary grins.

"Your friends?" he asks me.

"More or less," I tell him.

He laughs.

"They seem okay," he says.

"Yeah," I tell him, "don't they?"

"You're not embarrassed?" he asks me. "About them seeing you with me?"

"No," I tell him, blushing at the thought.

He smiles and looks into my eyes.

"They'll get used to it," he says.

I don't know what to say to that.

I don't want to tell Gary that Marlene won't have to get used to seeing us together because the next time I run into her I'm going to wring her neck.

And I definitely don't want to say, *Oh, by the way, in case I haven't mentioned it, I have to be home by twelve o'clock Saturday night.*

But I *do* have to say something.

So I say, "I've got to go."

As I say it, I'm kind of half hoping that Gary will ask me if I'd like him to walk me home. But I guess he's got something else to do because all he says is, "Yeah, me too."

Which is kind of disappointing, even if I was only half hoping.

"See you tomorrow," he says.

"Okay," I tell him.

"And Saturday night," he says.

Until twelve o'clock, I think, as I nod my cowardly head and say, "Yeah."

He looks into my eyes and squeezes my hand. I look into his eyes and squeeze his hand. And then, at the exact same moment, we both let go.

We don't say good-bye. I just stand there for a second, watching Gary as he walks to the door.

As he looks back at me and smiles and goes back into school, I turn and look across the parking lot— just in time to see Marlene's Toyota scooting out the back way.

But as I set out walking across the parking lot, I don't mind that I'm not riding with Marlene and Janice and Toby and Gayle.

The fact is, I'm kind of glad about it. Because frankly I'd rather walk and be alone with my thoughts and feel Gary's hand holding mine all the way home.

Thirteen

I'm in the kitchen, making myself a peanut butter and honey sandwich to get me through to the next commercial break in the *Monday Night Movie,* when the phone rings.

I figure it's Marlene, who I haven't called since I got home from school because I'm still so pissed about her blabbing that I'm not sure that I want to talk to her.

Taking my time, I saunter over to the phone and lift the receiver and say hello.

"Remind me never to talk to Toby again," says Marlene.

"Never talk to Toby again," I remind her.

"She swore she wouldn't say anything," she tells me.

I decide to play dumb.

"About what?" I ask her.

"When I drove her home after school," she says, "before I dropped her off, she invited me to a party at her house Saturday night."

"Really?" I say.

"Yeah," says Marlene. "So I told her I didn't know if I could come. It depends on what Dwyer wants to do."

"Everything does," I say.

Marlene doesn't hear me.

"Yeah," she says. "But then I asked her who else was coming to her party, and she says, 'I don't know.' I'm only the second person she's invited. So I say, 'Who was the first?' and she tells me you.

"Well . . . I could have killed her! I mean, I don't know why she did it—why she made up this whole thing about throwing a party and then invited you to it, just so you'd say no—unless she was just trying to get me into trouble with you.

"I mean, why would she want to get it out of you when I'd already told her?"

"Told her what?" I ask her.

"She said this thing to me," says Marlene. "This was this afternoon, after lunch, after gym class.

"We'd just come out of the showers and everybody was getting dressed, except for Janice, who was parading around the locker room in just these bikini briefs that say HOT on one cheek and STUFF on the other.

"So Janice is bopping around—HOT/STUFF/HOT/STUFF—and everybody's cracking jokes about her having the best read ass in school and everything, and Janice is laughing.

"So I say something to Toby about how I really feel sorry for Janice because of how she obviously doesn't have a lot of respect for herself.

"And Toby says, 'Well, I wouldn't feel too sorry about her getting sick Saturday night, if I were you.'

"So I said what did she mean by that? And she said, 'Never mind.'

"And I said she couldn't just say something like that and then not tell me what she meant by it.

" 'I can't tell you,' she says—because it's a secret that she heard from Gayle, and she's promised not to say anything to anybody."

"So you asked her if it was about Dwyer," I guess.

"Yeah," says Marlene. "How did you know?"

"Just guessing," I tell her. "And . . .?"

"And Toby says she can't say," says Marlene. "But the way that she's looking at me, I know it's something about Dwyer. So I had to find out what Toby had heard, right? Wouldn't you?"

"So you traded with her," I say. "Gayle's secret for mine."

"Everybody was going to find out anyhow!" says Marlene. "By Saturday night, anyway. I made Toby swear she'd keep her mouth shut until then. It was only a couple of days."

"Yeah," I say. "I can see how you'd expect a friend to be able to keep her mouth shut for at least that long."

"Yeah," says Marlene. "But you know Toby. She can't keep a secret any longer than Janice can keep a drink down. So I guess I should have known.

"But I had to find out about Dwyer and Janice," she says. "That's what I guessed it was about, what Gayle told Toby. You can understand that, right? How I had to find out?"

She waits for me to tell her that I understand. And the truth is, I do. But I'm not about to admit it.

"So what did she tell you?" I ask her. "What did you get for your thirty pieces of silver?"

"Oh," she says, like I've hurt her feelings, "don't be mad!"

"I'm trying not to be," I tell her. "But it isn't easy."

"Keep trying," she says. "Okay?"

"Yeah," I say. "So what did she tell you?"

Marlene sighs.

"Nothing really," she says.

"Great!" I say.

"Just that Gayle told her she thought that Janice probably got sick on purpose Saturday night, so Dwyer could offer to drive her home—that the two of them probably had the whole thing worked out that way. Can you imagine?"

Yes, I think. But I don't say it.

"And Toby believed it," says Marlene. "Isn't that incredible?"

"Incredible," I say.

But possible, I think.

"So I'm sorry," says Marlene. "Really. That's what I called to say. I'm really sorry. And if you want to hate me, it's all right. I'll understand.

"But," she says, "if you're willing to forgive me . . ."

I sigh.

"I'll tell you what," I say. "I'll trust you with one more secret, but you have to swear to me that you won't tell anybody, because if it gets out, everybody's going to think I'm a real jerk, okay?"

"Okay," says Marlene. "I swear."

"Okay," I tell her. "I forgive you."

Marlene laughs—a long, hard laugh—like she's really relieved.

And then, practically gushing gratitude, she says, "Thank you."

So, just to cut the calories, I say, "Go to hell!" and I wait to see if Marlene breaks up.

And the second that I hear her laugh, just to prove that things are back to normal between us, I slam down the phone on her.

Fourteen

Saturday night at nine-thirty sharp, I leave Mr. Schwed's office, where I've been cashing in for the day, and head for the lobby. I'm so nervous about tonight, I'm taking big gulps of air to fight off the shakes.

The thing is, I never did get around to telling Gary that I had to be home by twelve tonight, although I really meant to. I *did*. In fact, every time I bumped into Gary, all week long, I told myself I *ought to*. But I *never did*, because I also kept telling myself I *might not have to*.

I mean, it's possible that Gary will want to take me home before twelve anyway without my ever mentioning it, although—to be honest—it isn't very likely.

What's likely is, Gary and I will be at Charlie's, dancing or sharing a pizza, and it will get to be eleven-thirty and a quarter to twelve, and I'll be panicking about how late it's getting, and Gary won't be thinking about anything more than the next dance or the next slice of pizza.

And then, when it gets to be ten of twelve and five of twelve, I won't have any choice. *I'll have to tell him!*

That's the way it's likely to go.

And that's what I'm so nervous about. And why

it's taking me forever to get from Mr. Schwed's office to the lobby. And why I'm gulping for air like a beached whale.

But that's not the only reason I'm nervous. It's also got something to do with the way I look. *I look ridiculous!*

I mean, it took me forever to decide what to wear tonight, but somehow, I wound up wearing a short denim jacket over a sleeveless, red cotton jersey and a matching denim skirt that's no wider than a dish towel—so that you can see my legs all the way up to the middle of my chunky little thighs—and white leather boots.

I mean, here I am, about to go out on the biggest date of my life with the sexiest human being that I've ever met, and I look like some dopey model in a mail-order catalogue who's trying to pass herself off as Miss Teen Tramp.

Gary's going to laugh, I know it! I mean, when I walk out the door and he gets a look at me, he's going to just double over, he'll be laughing so hard. And then, he'll just straighten up and walk over to his car and hop into it and take off.

I mean, I can practically hear the screech of his tires, burning rubber and—over the roar of his engine—his laughter, echoing off into the night.

I stop at the door that leads out into the lobby. I take off my denim jacket and drape it over my arm. *But that looks ridiculous, too!*

Telling myself, *What's the use?*, I put my jacket back on and take a deep breath and propel myself out the door, straight into the jaws of Whatever Lies Ahead.

Gary! He's what lies ahead. Just ahead.

He isn't waiting for me in front of the theatre,

like I expected. He's waiting for me in the lobby. And as soon as I see him, I break up.

Because Gary's wearing a short denim jacket, denim jeans, and a bright red shirt.

I mean, except for the fact that he's wearing Nikes instead white leather boots, he's dressed like my twin! I mean, the two of us together, we look like a rock band!

Gary sees it too—how we're dressed alike—and he laughs.

"I like your taste," he says.

And I laugh.

"What happened to G.I. Joe?" I ask him.

"Oh," he says, "I gave him the night off."

And he takes my hand.

And a minute later, we're in Gary's car, heading out to Charlie's, and the radio's playing soft rock, and the cool night air is blowing in the windows, and I'm sitting beside Gary, wondering how I could have felt so nervous about going out with somebody that I feel so incredibly comfortable with.

"I'm impressed," I tell Gary.

"With my driving?" he asks.

"With *what* you're driving," I tell him.

"Oh," he says, "you're *that* kind of girl!"

"What kind is that?" I ask him.

He smiles and says, "Discerning."

"Oh, yes," I tell him. "I'm famous for my discernment."

He glances over at me and says, "You look pretty good in a miniskirt too."

I blush in spite of myself and say, "Thank you."

"My pleasure," he says.

And he smiles at me.

And I cross my legs.

And he laughs.

And I say, "Is your mother back?"

It's the first thing that comes into my head.

And Gary looks at me like, what am I asking him about his mother for?

"Because it's nice of her to give you the car," I say. "If she *is*, I mean. Back."

"Oh," he says. "Yeah."

But suddenly Gary isn't smiling anymore.

I guess I shouldn't have asked him about his mother.

"No," he says. "She isn't back."

"Oh," I say, hoping that will be the end of it.

"She isn't coming back," he says.

Jesus! I think. *Now I've done it!*

But all I say is, "Oh," like I'm sorry, and we don't have to talk about it anymore, if he doesn't want to.

But he wants to.

"Nobody knows," he says.

"I won't tell anybody," I promise.

Gary smiles at me.

"I know," he says.

It's kind of a sad smile.

"It's pretty heavy," he says.

"It must be," I tell him.

"I mean, I don't know if it's for good," he says, "but . . ."

He shrugs.

"She just couldn't get used to living here," he says. "She tried. But she's used to, you know, being with her friends and going out to the theatre and to restaurants and everything. She said she felt like she was suffocating here."

"God!" I say, because I don't know what else to say. I mean, what do you say?

"She left two weeks ago," he says, like he's

confessing, like he's embarrassed because he told me that his mother was just away for the weekend.

"Oh?" I say, not like I'm surprised, which I am, I admit, but more like I'm just curious.

Gary nods.

"It was supposed to be just for a visit," he says, "like I told you. But once she got to New York, she decided to stay."

I wish I knew what to say—what I *could* say that would make Gary feel better. I can see that he's really upset. But the best I can come up with is, "How's your father?"

Pretty lame, I know, but it actually seems to help because Gary smiles and shakes his head and says, "Unsinkable."

"What do you mean?" I ask him.

"I mean it's probably got him all torn up," he says. "But he'd never show it. He's too proud."

"And you're proud of him," I say.

"Yeah," he says. "He's quite a guy."

"He must be," I say, "the way you talk about him."

"Yeah," he says. "But anyway, I would have told you before. About my mother. But I didn't want to pile all my problems on you."

"Oh," I say, "that's okay. Everybody needs somebody."

"But," he says, "I didn't want to lie to you either, because . . ."

He looks over at me, looks into my eyes.

"Because I really like you," he says.

I feel tears coming to my eyes—that's how happy I am, how good I feel—but I don't turn away to hide them. I look into Gary's eyes, and I say, "I really like you, too."

And Gary smiles and says, "Great!"

And I smile and say, "Yeah."

"I mean, it's great that we both feel alike," he says. "But we've definitely got to stop dressing alike."

"Yeah," I say, and I sigh, like I'm disappointed. And then, like I'm shrugging it off, I say, "I don't look so hot in khaki anyway."

Gary laughs and says, "You'd look hot in anything."

I laugh and say, "My mother was right about you."

"That I'm smooth?" he says.

I shake my head.

"That you're very attractive," I tell him.

He smiles and says, "You should see me dance."

"I can't wait," I tell him.

But the way it works out, I have to.

Fifteen

When we get to Charlie's, the jukebox is blaring, and the dance floor is packed, and the whole place is swarming with kids. But who do I see, the second we walk in the door?

Marlene and Dwyer. Right. The two of them are sitting at a table between the counter where you pick up your food and the dance floor.

At first, I'm kind of surprised to see them because, the last I heard, Marlene was planning on going to the party that Toby wound up throwing at her house tonight.

But I guess Dwyer must have had other plans, because here they are, although—to be honest— Marlene doesn't look like exactly thrilled about it. In fact, she looks lousy, like she's really unhappy, and when she finally notices me, I can see by the way she smiles at me that something's wrong.

"Isn't that your friend?" asks Gary.

He has to shout a little to be heard over the jukebox, which is bellowing out some song by U-2—the name of which I can't tell you because they all sound alike to me.

But I nod and say, "Yes. Marlene. I have to say hello. Do you mind?"

"No," he says. "But we don't have to sit with them, do we?"

Which surprises me.

I ask Gary, "Do you know Dwyer?"

He nods and says, "About as well as I want to."

"I know what you mean," I tell him.

He smiles and takes my hand, and we walk over to Marlene's table.

When we get there, we say hello and, right away, Marlene says, "I've got to go to the bathroom."

From the way she looks at me when she says it, I can tell that she wants me to go with her. So, as she gets up from the table, I look at Gary and say, "Me, too."

Gary doesn't look all that happy about being stuck with Dwyer.

Who would?

But nonetheless, he says, "Okay. I'll wait here." And he sits down with Dwyer.

And Marlene and I take off for the ladies' room.

Sixteen

The second we get to the ladies' room, as soon as I close the door behind us, Marlene bursts into tears.

Right away, I put my arms around her and ask her what's wrong. But Marlene pushes me away and like she's accusing me of something she says, "Did you know about Janice?"

"No," I say. Because I didn't, and I still don't. "What about her?" I ask.

"She *let him!*" she sobs.

God! I think. *How could she?!*

"Are you sure?" I say.

"Yes!" she cries. "Last Saturday night!"

"How do you know?" I ask her.

"Toby told me," she says.

"Oh," I say, "that's just Toby."

"No!" she cries. "Gayle told her. And Janice told Gayle."

"That doesn't make it true," I tell her.

"He *admits it!*" she sobs.

"Jesus!"

"He says if I won't give it to him, then it's none of my business where he gets it."

"God!" I say. "What a pig!"

"No!" she says. "He's *right!*"

I can't believe she means what she's saying.

88

"He is?" I ask her.

"I don't know," she says. "I just . . . I *love* him!"

"Still?" I ask her.

"Yes!" she sobs.

I try to put my arms around her again, and this time, she lets me.

"Oh, Marlene," I tell her. "I'm so sorry."

I hold her close and feel her tears against my cheek.

"I'm not going to give him up," she says.

"Do you want my opinion?" I ask her.

"No!" she says as she pulls away from me again. "Yes."

I take her at her word.

"He's using Janice to blackmail you," I tell her.

"I *know* that!" she cries.

"You can't let him," I tell her.

"I *know!*" she says. "But I can't give him up either. I *love* him!"

I want to say *Why?* but I don't, because it doesn't matter why.

"What am I going to do?" she cries.

"Drive a stake through his heart," I suggest.

"I'm serious!" she says.

"So am I," I tell her. "God, Marlene! If you let him just to keep him, you'll end up losing him anyway. You know that."

"No, I don't," she says.

"That's how it works," I tell her.

"Not always," she says.

"No," I admit. "I guess not. But what about you? How are you going to feel, if you . . . ?"

She laughs.

She's still got tears streaming down her face, but

she laughs through them and she says, "Like a woman."

"Yeah," I say. "But what kind of woman?"

Marlene just looks at me for a second, and then she says, "Wish me luck?"

"I can't," I tell her.

She nods.

"You'll be the last," she says.

"I hate him," I tell her. "I really do."

"You always have," she says.

"Not like I do now," I tell her.

"You go ahead," she says. "I want to wash up."

"Please," I say, "don't."

"Maybe I won't," she says.

"He's such a shit."

"I love you," she says.

"Please, Marlene?"

"Tell him I'll be out in a minute," she says.

I shake my head.

"Let him figure it out for himself," I tell her. "I'm not talking to him."

She smiles.

"I probably won't," she says. "I'm too scared."

"If you want a ride home . . ."

She shakes her head.

"Any time you say," I tell her.

"Thanks," she says.

"He doesn't deserve you."

"Have you ever been in love?" she asks me.

Maybe, I think. *Maybe I am, right now.* But I'm not sure. And even if I was, I wouldn't have the heart to tell Marlene. Not now.

So I just shake my head.

"Lucky you," says Marlene.

And then, like there's nothing more to say, she

turns and walks over to the sink, hangs her head and turns on both faucets full blast.

I feel rotten, leaving her like this.

But I remind myself that it's her life and, saying a silent prayer for her, I turn and walk out the door.

Seventeen

Everything's the way I left it. As I come out of the ladies' room, the jukebox is still blaring and the dance floor is still swarming with kids. But now, it all seems like it's too much.

I'd like to kill Dwyer. And Janice, too.

Well, not really. But talk about lowlifes! God! The two of them! *Where's Gary?*

As I squeeze through the crowd and make my way back to the table where I left Gary, I see Dwyer—the shit—still sitting there, but *I don't see Gary!*

I'm about to panic. I mean, things are bad enough without—Someone laughs behind me. Recognizing the laugh, I spin around and see Gary coming out of the men's room with Alan Sinclair.

I'm relieved and surprised. I guess I shouldn't be—surprised, I mean—because Gary seems to know practically everybody—Brian Avery, Wayne Shuster, Dwyer—but hardly anybody knows Alan Sinclair.

I mean, everybody knows who Alan Sinclair *is* because he's just fifteen, and he's already the hottest guitar player in town. But nobody knows who he *really* is, because he spends all his time either stoned on music or stoned on pot or both, and you can hardly make him out through the haze he's always in.

As he walks up to me, as if he were really impressed to meet the girl that Gary has been telling him such wonderful things about, Alan looks at me and says, "Is this *her?*"

Alan's teasing of course, but Gary just smiles like he enjoys being teased about me.

"That's her," he says.

Alan squints at me.

"I know you," he says.

He turns to Gary.

"I know her," he says.

He turns back to me.

"Don't I?" he says.

I laugh.

"I've seen you around school," I tell him.

"You sure it wasn't at the Grammy Awards?" he asks me. "There was a girl that looked just like you. The spitting image."

He laughs.

"Spitting image," he says and then, turning to Gary, he says, "What the hell is *that* supposed to mean?"

Gary laughs.

"I don't know," he says. "I didn't say it."

Alan reaches up—he's only about five-foot-two or something—and he puts his hands on Gary's shoulders and he looks Gary straight in the eye and totally serious, he says, "I hope you never have to."

Gary breaks up.

Alan hugs him.

"May the force be with you," he says.

"You, too," he tells me.

And then he's gone.

"Funny guy," says Gary as we watch Alan disappearing into the crowd.

"Yes," I agree. "But you know what's really funny?"

Gary looks at me.

"How I've lived here all my life," I tell him, "and you just got here, but whenever we bump into anybody, *you're* always introducing *me*."

Gary laughs.

"Why is that?" I ask him.

"Because I'm proud of you," he says.

Which is sweet, but not what I meant.

"No," I say.

"How's Marlene?" he asks me.

Marlene! I think. For a second, I'd almost forgotten. I guess I wanted to.

But now I heave a sigh and tell Gary, "Not so good."

He looks over at Dwyer.

"Does she go out with him?" he asks me.

"Yes," I tell him.

"Why?" he asks me.

I don't know why. Because he's good looking in a piggy sort of way? Because he's a Catholic and so is she? Because she's got lousy taste in men?

It beats me. Which is what I'm about to tell Gary, when I notice Marlene coming out of the ladies' room and heading our way.

She looks better than she did when I left her a minute ago, but she also looks like Joan of Arc, marching to the stake.

As she gets near us, she gives me a tight little smile and chirps out a tight little, "Hi."

"We're ready to go," I remind her, "whenever you are."

Gary looks at me, but he doesn't say anything.

And neither does Marlene.

She just keeps on smiling and keeps on walking, all the way back to her table.

"What's that all about?" Gary asks me.

God! The smile on Dwyer's face when he sees Marlene coming! It makes my skin crawl!

"Hello," says Gary, waving his fingers in front of my eyes. "Is anybody home?"

"Oh," I say, remembering his question. "I told her to ditch Dwyer."

"Oh," he says.

"Do you mind?" I ask him.

Gary shakes his head.

"What are friends for?" he says.

"Thanks," I tell him.

He smiles.

"Want to dance?" he says.

I heave a sigh.

"Honestly?" I ask him.

"Honestly," he says.

I shake my head.

"I really don't feel much like it," I tell him.

"I'm not that good," he assures me, as if I were worried about keeping up with him on the dance floor, which makes me laugh, in spite of everything, because I'm a pretty good dancer, if I do say so myself, and—now that I think about it—Gary's a pretty wonderful guy.

"Prove it," I tell him.

Gary smiles.

"I'll do my worst," he says, and he takes my hand and leads me onto the dance floor.

"Brown Sugar" is playing on the jukebox when we arrive, but we don't jump right into it.

We start out slow, moving easy, smiling at each

other and looking into each other's eyes. Then, after a second, when we've both got the feel of it, we begin picking up the pace. And then, in what seems like no time at all, the music takes over, and suddenly we're going full out, throwing ourselves into it, giving ourselves up to it.

And God! Gary's so good, so free, so hot! And me—I'm right with him, every step of the way, responding to his every move, anticipating his every move. And before I know it, it's almost as if I were him, and he were me, and our minds and bodies were one.

And God! We're so good, so free, so hot!

I've never felt . . . If Gary touched me now . . . If he kissed me . . .

Applause . . . People clapping . . . God!

Everybody's standing all around us, looking at us, applauding us! I can't imagine why, until suddenly, it strikes me—*The music has stopped, the song has ended, and I'm still dancing!* We *are. No!*

Gary's applauding too. He's standing there, next to me, smiling at me and applauding!

I want to die, I'm so embarrassed. I feel *almost naked!*

But Gary doesn't seem embarrassed at all. He reaches out and takes my hand and turns to the crowd and bows and then, straightening up, he directs the crowd's applause to me.

And suddenly, as if I were seeing it through Gary's eyes, it all seems so funny.

I look over at Gary, and I laugh, and then I turn to the crowd, and I curtsy.

And then, as the music starts up again and everybody goes back to dancing, Gary puts his arm around me and whisks me off the dance floor.

I can't help laughing. I'm so happy and feeling so good, and Gary's arm around me feels so right.

"I told you I wasn't that good," he says, as if he wasn't.

"You lied," I tell him.

"No," he says. "You brought out the best in me. I've never been anywhere near that good before."

"Really?" I ask him.

"Never," he says.

"Me, neither," I tell him.

He smiles.

"You want to get some air?" he says.

And suddenly, it hits me. As I turn and sweep my eyes over the crowd, I say, "Have you seen Marlene?"

"She left," says Gary.

A chill goes through me.

"She did?"

"While we were dancing," he says.

I don't want to believe it.

"You saw her?"

"Them," he says. "I saw them heading for the door."

"Are you sure?"

Gary nods and says, "They had their arms around each other."

Oh, God! I think. *She's going to do it!*

Gary puts his finger under my chin and turns my face to his and looks into my eyes.

"Tell me," he says.

I shake my head.

"I can't," I tell him.

"You can tell me anything," he says.

"I know," I tell him. "But Marlene wouldn't want me to."

Gary smiles.

"Everybody tells you their secrets," he says.

Which—now that I think of it—is true.

"I'm thinking about becoming a priest," I tell him.

Gary laughs and shakes his head.

"You'd never pass the physical," he says.

The way he's looking at me, I'm not sure how long I could stick to my vow of chastity either. But thinking about chastity reminds me of Marlene again, which bums me out, totally.

As if he could read my mind, Gary says, "Do you want to go?"

"You mean home?" I ask him.

"Wherever," he says.

"What time is it?" I ask him.

He smiles at me and looks at his watch.

"Ten-thirty," he says.

I can't believe it. I mean, it feels like the middle of the night to me, but to Gary it must seem like the night has just begun.

"Don't you want to stay?" I ask him.

He shakes his head.

"I just want to be with you," he says.

"Are you sure?"

He smiles.

"Positive," he says.

"Okay," I tell him. "If you're sure."

He smiles and takes my hand and leads me off through the crowd.

"Where to?" he says as we get to the door.

As we go out the door, I say, "Wherever."

Eighteen

I can't stop thinking about Marlene and Dwyer. As Gary and I walk out into Charlie's parking lot, they're what's on my mind.

I know they shouldn't be. I should be thinking about Gary and me. And getting home by twelve. And where we're going now. And what we're going to do, once we get to wherever we're going now. But I keep seeing Marlene and Dwyer.

I see them together in the backseat of Dwyer's car. I see Dwyer all over Marlene. I see tears streaming down Marlene's face. I see . . .

I tell myself to cut it out. There's a moon shining out on the lake and a million stars in the sky and this really incredible guy is holding my hand in his.

But none of that means a thing to me, because I can't stop thinking about Marlene and Dwyer. I can't stop seeing them . . .

"Police," says Gary.

Squinting my eyes against the sudden glare of headlights, I say, "What?"

"Police," he says.

I see a police car pulling into the parking lot.

"Oh," I say. "Yeah."

As we stand watching, the police car brakes to a stop. The door swings open and Officer Glenn Van Dyke climbs out from behind the wheel.

"Van Dyke," says Gary.

"You know him?" I ask.

Of course he does, I tell myself. *He knows everybody.*

"No," says Gary.

So I'm wrong.

"But I've heard about him," he says.

Which isn't that surprising, since everybody has. Van Dyke is the worst. He's always pulling kids over, giving them a hard time, searching their cars—just for the fun of it. And just for kicks, if he catches you with something stupid, like a broken taillight or something, he'll haul you off to jail. That's the kind of guy he is.

A lot of people say that if Glenn Van Dyke's father weren't the chief of police and he hadn't gotten Glenn his job on the police force then, sooner or later, he would have wound up arresting him.

Which is probably true. But anyway, as he passes by us, Van Dyke doesn't say anything. He just looks us over, like we've got no right to live, and he keeps on going.

I can just imagine the pall that's going to settle over the crowd at Charlie's when Van Dyke walks in the door. I can just see all of the underage kids, scurrying to get rid of their drinks.

"This is it," says Gary.

He opens the door to his car for me.

I say, "Thanks," and climb inside.

Gary walks around the front of the car and climbs in behind the wheel.

He starts up the car and then, turning to me, he says, "You want to just drive around the lake for a while?" and I say, "Okay"—although to be honest, I'm a little nervous about what might happen if Gary decides to park.

There are lots of places to park around the lake, and a lot of kids do. And normally, I guess I wouldn't mind if that's what Gary wanted to do. But right this minute, I'm kind of afraid.

It's because of Marlene and Dwyer, I guess. Not that I think Gary would try to get me to do anything that I didn't want to do, because I don't think he would. But even just kissing—I don't know—it would be like bringing up a subject that I don't want to think about, right now, the subject of Marlene and . . .

"Music?"

"Yes," I say. "That'd be nice."

While I've been talking to myself, Gary's pulled out of Charlie's parking lot and onto the little two-lane road that runs around the lake.

Now, he turns on his radio and dials up some softly-rocking driving-around-the-lake music.

"How's that?" he asks me.

"Great," I say.

We listen for a while, neither of us saying anything, just driving.

But then, after a while, Gary says, "Do you feel like talking?"

"Yeah," I say.

"But not about Marlene," he guesses.

I shake my head.

Gary nods.

"So tell me," he says, "what do you want to be when you grow up?"

I laugh.

But Gary's serious. So I tell him what I know about what I want to be when I grow up, which isn't that much.

I mean, I don't want to tell him that if I could be anything I wanted to be, I'd like to do something with movies. Aside from selling candy at them, I mean.

I mean—I don't know—I *know* I could never be an actress or anything. I'm not that pretty or that outgoing. But sometimes, when I'm watching a movie, the pictures up on the screen seem to flow from shot to shot and scene to scene in the same way that they do when I picture things in my imagination—like when I'm imagining how things might be, if things weren't the way they were. And when that happens, I sometimes think that maybe I could write movies or direct them or something.

But like I said, I don't want to tell any of that to Gary.

I mean, I've never really told it to anybody, because I'm afraid they'd laugh at me. And who could blame them?

So instead of telling Gary about my dreams of glory, I tell him the way that my life's most likely going to go.

"I don't know," I tell him. "I guess I'll go to college. To Syracuse, probably, because it's close. And it's supposed to be pretty good. And I'll get a well-rounded education. Like everybody's supposed to. And meet some nice enough guy. Maybe a lawyer—a law student. And he'll fall in love with me, of course. And we'll both graduate at the same time. Me from college, and him from law school. And then we'll get married. And move back here. And he'll set up his law practice. And I'll work in his office, until he gets established and I get pregnant. And we'll have two kids, and I'll raise them, because by then, he'll be too busy with work to help. And every Sunday, we'll take my mother and the kids and go up to the country club for dinner. And we'll sit at our regular table and wave across the room to our regular friends and have a regular old good time. Until our kids grow up and leave us, and we get real old and die.''

"Jesus!" says Gary. "That sounds awful."

"Yeah," I say. "Doesn't it?"

Gary smiles.

"It doesn't have to be that way," he says.

I nod and say, "I know."

"You can make it anything you want," he says.

"Do you really think so?" I ask him.

Gary doesn't say anything for a second. He just looks over at me, as if he were studying me. And then, as if he's made up his mind, he nods and says, "I know so."

And for that moment, at least, I believe him—I believe that I can be anything I want to be—a movie star, a writer, a director, Woody Allen—because Gary believes that I can.

I'm thinking, *Maybe I could tell him,* when Gary says, "Hey! Have you ever been to The Champions?"

"No," I tell him.

I don't know what he's talking about.

"Oh," he says, "you've got to see it."

"I do?"

"Oh, yeah," he says. "It's a must!"

And the next thing I know, he's swinging the car off the road and heading straight for a bunch of trees at the edge of the woods.

For a second I think we're going to crash right into them. But then, at the last minute, Gary's headlights pick up a pair of crumbling stone pillars among the trees and, shooting between them, we go bouncing down a driveway overgrown with weeds, and then—passing by a faded sign that reads WELCOME TO THE CAMPIONS—we continue on, plunging down the driveway into the deepening darkness of the woods.

And I'm panicking. I'm thinking, *Oh, my God! We're going to park!* But all I say is, "How'd you know about this place?"

And Gary laughs and says, "I told you. I'm an explorer."

"What is it?" I ask him.

"*Was* it," he says.

And just then we break out of the woods and into a clearing and there, set high up on a rolling lawn and looking out over the moonlit lake, I see this huge building, like a hotel or something, but made out of wood and very old and very pretty.

"Wow!" I say. "It's like a fairytale."

Gary smiles and says, "Yeah. It used to be a private home. An estate. But Mr. Campion lost all his money in the stock market crash, and they had to turn it into a hotel. But then," he says, "World War II came along and wiped that out. And since then, as far as I can tell, nobody's been here but me. Until now."

Pulling the car as close to the lake as he can get, he brakes to a stop. And he kills the lights. And he turns off the engine.

And at that moment, as the darkness and silence rush in on me, I think, *This is it!*

But Gary says, "Come on."

And as he climbs out of the car, I heave a sigh of relief. *Or is it disappointment?*

I don't know which. All I know is, without waiting for Gary to walk around the car and open the door for me, I open the door and climb out.

"Isn't this great?" says Gary.

He walks up to me and takes my hand.

"Yeah," I say.

"Come on," he says and, tugging my hand, he starts leading me down to the lake.

By the light of the moon, we make our way down to the water and along the shore to an old wooden dock that's built out over the lake.

As we reach the dock, I ask Gary, "Is it safe?"

"No," he says. But then, he smiles and says, "Come on."

So I do. Holding his hand, I follow him out onto the dock.

We've only gone about four steps when Gary stops and turns back to me and smiles and says, "This is about as far as I've explored."

"Here?" I say.

"Here," he says, and still holding hands, we sit down on the edge of the dock and dangle our feet out over the water.

And it's beautiful—the moonlight dancing on the lake, the trees balancing along its edge, the twinkling lights of lakeside cottages peeking out from among the trees, the call of night birds, the splashing of waves along the shore, their lazy thumping beneath the dock . . . and Gary's hand, holding mine.

Neither of us says anything for quite a while.

But then after a while, because I'm really curious, I say, "What about you? When you grow up, I mean. What do you want to be?"

Like he's kidding but not quite, Gary smiles and says, "Very successful."

I laugh and say, "Yes. But at what?"

"Oh," he says. "I haven't figured that out yet."

I laugh at that too.

"I might be a rock star," he says.

"Oh," I say. "That would be nice. I didn't know you played. Or do you just sing?"

He laughs and says, "Neither."

"Hmm," I say. "That's going to make it rough."

"I write," he says.

"Songs?" I ask him.

Gary smiles and says, "That's what they're supposed to be. When *they* grow up."

"Really?" I say.

I mean, I thought he was just kidding around, but . . .

"Yeah," he says. "Me and Alan."

"Sinclair?"

"Yes," he says. "But so far, it's mostly Alan. He writes the music."

"And you write the words?" I ask him.

"And do the choreography," he says.

"You dance?"

Gary laughs and says, "I'm just kidding."

"You don't write songs?" I ask him.

"No," he says. "I mean, yes. I do. With Alan."

"Can I hear one?" I ask him.

He smiles and shakes his head and says, "You're too young to die."

"Oh," I plead, "come on!"

He smiles and shakes his head and says, "Not yet."

"When?" I ask him.

"When I get one that's good enough," he says.

"For what?" I ask him.

"For you," he says.

He says it like he really means it, and he looks into my eyes, and I think, *I love you, Gary!* but I say, "No. Seriously."

106

And without taking his eyes from mine, Gary nods and says, "Seriously."

And although I can scarcely breathe, somehow I manage to say, "Well, I'll be ready, whenever you are."

Gary smiles and says, "It could take a while."

I smile and say, "I'm not in any hurry." But then, almost before the words are out of my mouth—because I've just remembered, *I've got to be home by twelve*—I say, "What time is it?"

Gary laughs. And then, letting go of my hand, he lifts his wrist and turns the face of his watch into the moonlight.

"Eleven-thirty," he says.

Which is a relief.

"Oh," I say.

"Why?" he asks me.

I shrug and tell him, "I just wondered."

Gary smiles and looks into my eyes again, and he says, "Did you ever notice how people's eyes look different in the moonlight?"

I don't answer—I can't!—because the way Gary's looking at me, the way it makes me feel, I don't have any idea what he's talking about!

"Like your eyes," he says. "In daylight they're the palest blue, so quiet and peaceful. But now, in the moonlight, they're deep blue and dappled with gold."

And he leans to kiss me.

"Gary . . ."

And he kisses me. Tenderly. But I'm too scared to let it last.

As gently as I can, I break it off. "Please . . ."

Gary doesn't understand.

"I want to," I tell him. "I want you to kiss me. And I want to kiss you. Honest I do."

107

He just looks at me.

"It isn't *you!*" I tell him. "It's just . . . I'm having a bad night."

"You are?" he says.

He looks disappointed.

I nod and say, "I'm sorry. Because I really do like you. More than like you."

Gary smiles and says, "That's good."

I look into his eyes and say, "I'm not a tease either, if that's what you're thinking."

He laughs and says, "That's good, too."

"But . . ."

"Marlene?" he guesses.

I nod.

"You're going steady?" he guesses. "You and Marlene?"

I have to laugh at that.

"I mean, if you *are* . . ." he says.

I punch him in the arm, up near his shoulder where it really hurts.

"Ow!" he says.

"Cut it out!" I tell him.

"I just thought . . ." he says.

I punch him again, in the same place as before.

"Ow!!" he says.

"Do you think that just because a girl doesn't want to kiss you, she has to be gay?" I ask him.

He *thinks* about it!

Which breaks me up.

"Probably," he says.

"Well," I tell him, "it isn't so!"

Gary smiles and says, "That's *very* good."

And he leans to kiss me.

And I let him.

And he kisses me. Very lovingly.

And then he leans back away from me. And he smiles.

And I want him to kiss me again. And I'm afraid that he might. And I say, "Maybe we can come back here another night."

"Next Saturday?" he says.

Which—considering what a drag I'm being—is pretty surprising and completely wonderful.

"Sure," I say. "If you want to."

He smiles and says, "I want to."

"Okay," I tell him.

"And you won't be having a bad night?" he asks me. "Next Saturday?"

I laugh and say, "Probably not."

Gary smiles and says, "That's good enough for me."

"Come on," he says.

And he gets to his feet and offers me his hand and helps me up.

And then we just stand there for a second—the two of us, side by side and holding hands—looking out over the lake, admiring the night and the view.

And then, very quietly, so as not to shatter the hush of the night, Gary says, "It's a shame to waste all this on conversation."

I smile at him and say, "I like conversation."

He smiles at me and says, "Me, too. Up to a point."

I laugh and I say, "Me, too."

And Gary grins and squeezes my hand and says, "Come on."

Nineteen

Conversation on the way home from The Campions:
1. School.

Gary and I agree that it's mostly a drag, but a couple of teachers are really good, and they make what they teach pretty interesting.

2. Music.

Gary and I agree that it's the greatest, except maybe for movies, and that all kinds of it have things worth listening to, except for maybe ultra-modern classical music that doesn't have any melody and the most vicious heavy metal stuff.

3. Gary's songs.

I agree not to talk about them—to Gary or Alan or anybody else—until they're good enough to be worth talking about.

And Gary agrees—after I promise to keep his songwriting a secret—that I'll be the first person to hear his songs, when he thinks his songs are ready to be heard.

Twenty

"Do you mind if I get the door for you?"

We're just pulling up in front of my house.

"No," I say.

Gary says, "Good."

At first, it seems like an odd question. But as Gary climbs out of the car and moves around to get my door, it occurs to me that his getting the door for me *is* kind of old-fashioned.

I mean, it's sweet and everything, but it's also kind of *macho*, which makes me feel kind of *femmo* and *icko*.

So, when Gary opens the door for me and offers me his hand, I tell him, "As long as it's my turn, next time."

When he laughs and says, "Sure," I take his hand.

As he helps me out of the car, I say, "Thank you."

Gary smiles.

"My pleasure," he says.

I smile back at him and walk with him, hand in hand, up the walk to my front steps and up the steps to my front door.

As we reach the door, I turn to him and he turns to me, and we stand there, looking into each other's eyes.

And then, without a word and very slowly, still looking into my eyes, Gary leans down to me and finds my mouth with his and kisses me.

And very slowly, I open my mouth and slide my tongue between Gary's lips and into his mouth and over his tongue. And I press my body against his. And he presses his body against mine. And I feel his body, moving against me. And I feel his hand at my breast. And I feel myself . . . pulsing . . . throbbing . . . aching . . . moaning . . . And Gary . . . *Gary* . . .

"God!" he says.

He holds me tight against him.

"If you only knew how much . . ." he says.

"I have to go," I tell him.

But I don't move.

"Okay," he says.

And pulls me even closer to him and holds me even tighter and takes a deep, deep breath.

And then, as he releases his breath, he releases me.

And for a second, as I step back away from him, I'm so breathless and shaky, I'm afraid I'll collapse right there in front of him. And I guess I must look scared, too, because Gary reaches out to me and lifts my face to his and looks into my eyes and says, "Are you afraid of me?"

I shake my head.

"Not *you*," I tell him.

He smiles and says, "I'm not in any hurry."

I smile and say, "That's good."

He laughs. "So are you," he says, "You're terrific."

"I promised my mother I'd be home by twelve."

Gary looks at me, like he thinks I must be kidding. But when he sees that I'm not, he just nods and looks at his watch, smiles, and says, "You've still got two minutes."

"That's *very* good," I tell him.

And I kiss him. But not like before. I just kiss him, as lovingly as I know how to and end it, long before I want to.

And then, looking into his eyes, I say, "I've never loved anybody, before."

And before Gary can say anything, I fumble my way through the front door, and I stumble into the house, and I close the door behind me and, leaning back against it, I shout, "Mom?"

Twenty-one

I've never been in love before. In fact, I've never
even thought I was in love before.

There have been boys I liked and boys that I
liked the looks of. There's even been a few boys—
two or three—who I both liked *and* liked the looks
of. But I never kidded myself that I was in love
with any of them. And I never said the words to
anybody. Until just now.

I'm in love! It's huge! The feeling of being in
love, I mean. It's enormous!

I want to laugh and cry and sing and dance and
plaster it on a billboard and write it across the sky!

At the very least, I want to tell somebody about
it, right now.

I could tell my mother.

She's upstairs in her bedroom. A second ago,
when I closed the door and shouted "Mom?" she
called down to me, "Up here!" And right this
second, I feel this tremendous urge to shout back
up to her, "Guess what? I'm in love!"

I imagine her not answering for a second and then
walking out of her room and over to the top of the
stairs and looking down at me and smiling and
saying, "Oh, Angel! How wonderful!"

But who am I kidding?

If I told my mother that I was in love, she'd hit

the panic button, I know it. She'd think I was crazy, falling in love with somebody the first time I went out with him. It wouldn't make any sense to her. How could I possibly fall in love with somebody who I'd just met and barely knew? Somebody who she wasn't all that sure she approved of? Somebody as "smooth" as Gary Everson? Unless, of course, I'd been drugged and seduced. That might explain it.

Were you?

I can just see my mother asking me that. I can see her eyes widening as the thought dawns on her, and her hand reaching for the phone as she gets ready to call the police.

I can't tell her, I realize. Not yet. Not until she's gotten to know Gary a little better and learned to trust him a little more.

I call up the stairs, "I'm home!"

My mother calls back down to me, "Come on up. I'm watching a movie."

"Okay," I shout.

As I start climbing the stairs to my mother's room, I flash on Marlene. That's who I'd really like to tell.

Even though it's past midnight and Marlene's father would freak out if he heard the phone ringing, I'd still call Marlene right now, if I thought she was home. But I doubt that she is.

Marlene! I think. *God!* As I reach the top of the stairs, I close my eyes and send a message out into the night, *Wherever you are, if it isn't too late, for God's sake, don't!*

"How was it?"

My mother calls to me from her room.

I open my eyes and pull myself together and walk over to her door and look in. She's lying across her

115

bed, watching TV—Richard Dreyfus is clowning around in somebody's kitchen—and sipping red wine. As I step into the room, she sets her glass down on the floor and looks over at me.

"Okay," I tell her. "Fine. We went to Charlie's. Gary's a good dancer. How was yours?"

"The usual," she says. "Okay."

"Oh," I say. "What's Richard Dreyfus up to?"

"He's an inventor," she says. "Want to watch with me?"

"I don't think so," I tell her. "I think I'll just go to bed."

"Okay," she says. "Good night."

I say, "Good night," and head for the door.

As I walk down the hall to my room, my mother calls after me, "I'm glad you had a good time."

I call back to her, "Thanks."

As I walk into my room and begin getting undressed and ready for bed, I feel a little depressed—because of Marlene and my mother and how I'm in love but don't have anybody I can tell about it.

But by the time I've climbed into bed and switched off the light, I'm smiling again because, even if I don't have anybody I can tell about it, I'm in love, and suddenly, that's all I can think about.

So that's what I do. I lie there in my bed, smiling and thinking, *I'm in love! I'm in love!*—over and over again, all night long.

And when the phone rings the next morning, I'm surprised that it wakes me up because I'm still thinking, *I'm in love!* and I don't remember that I ever stopped.

But the second I hear the phone ringing, I know who it is. *It's Gary,* I tell myself. *It has to be!*

"Angelica?"

My mother calls to me from downstairs.

"It's Toby," she shouts.

Great! I think. *Gary's trying to reach me, and she's tieing up my line!* I'm about to shout, *I'll call her back,* but it suddenly occurs to me, *Maybe she's talked to Marlene.*

"Angelica?"

"Okay," I shout.

As I drag myself out of bed, I glance over at my alarm clock.

It's almost twelve! God! I've missed church again. My mother must have let me sleep, which was nice of her, but—Jesus!—I have to be at work by one!

"Angelica?"

"I've got it."

I pad over to my desk and plop down in my chair.

I shout, "Thanks, Mom," and pick up the phone and say, "Hi."

And Toby says, "Good *morning!*" like my sleeping this late is some kind of scandal.

Ignoring her insinuation, I say, "What's up?"

But Toby—being Toby—wants to know what's up with *me.* Specifically, she wants to know how things went with me and Gary last night. And what kind of guy Gary is. And where we went. And especially, what we did.

I tell her as little as I can, without looking like I've got something to hide. I tell her that we went to Charlie's. And Gary's very nice. And I had a great time.

"Are you going out with him again?" she asks me. "If he asks you?"

"Yeah," I tell her. "Next Saturday."

117

"Oh, yeah?" she says, like she isn't sure if she approves.

"Yeah," I tell her.

"Oh," she says, like something's bothering her, something that she wants to tell me about.

I can't imagine what it might be, and I don't really care, and I'd just as soon drop the whole subject of Gary and me, but my curiosity gets the best of me and, putting my better judgment aside, I say, "Okay. What is it?"

"Nothing," she says. "Only . . ."

I can feel myself starting to get angry.

"Only *what?*" I ask her.

"I don't know," she says. "But when Gayle told her brother who you were going out with . . ."

"Why'd she do that?" I ask her.

"I don't know," she says. "I guess he must have seen you and Gary around school. You've been with him enough!"

Enough for what? I wonder.

"Yeah," I say. "So what did Ronnie have to say?"

Not that I'm that interested in Ronnie Crosby's opinion of Gary.

I mean, Ronnie's okay, I guess, but as far as I know, he's not supposed to be any great judge of character.

"Nothing," says Toby.

I lose it.

"Nothing?!"

"Not really," she says. "He just made a face and said, 'Gary *Everson?*' Like he couldn't believe it."

"Why'd he do that?"

"I don't know," she says. "He just did."

"He probably doesn't even know Gary."

"Maybe that's why," says Toby. "Nobody does."

"*I* do," I tell her.

"Well . . . ." she says, as if my opinion doesn't count.

And then—before she can tell me what Ronnie's third cousin did when Ronnie told *him* who I was going out with—I say, "How was your party?"

"A disaster!" she says.

I smile and feel glad that Toby can't see me and then, guiltily, as if I really cared, I say, "How come?"

So Toby tells me about Janice—and how she spent the whole night waiting for Dwyer to show up, even though everybody knew that Dwyer was going out with Marlene.

"Why'd she do that?" I ask her.

"Because," says Toby, "according to what Janice told Gayle, Dwyer was supposed to break up with Marlene last night."

"What?"

"Yeah," she says. "According to Gayle, Dwyer was supposed to break up with Marlene, and then he was supposed to come over and pick up Janice at my house and spend the rest of the night with her. Well, not the *whole* rest of the night—although I wouldn't put it past either of them—but you know."

"But Dwyer didn't show up?" I ask her.

It's not really a question because, from the way Toby's talking, it's pretty obvious that he didn't. But even so, I'm hoping that I've got it wrong, and I'm praying that somehow, at the last minute,

119

Marlene came to her senses and told Dwyer to get lost.

But Toby says, "No. He didn't even call."

I get a sick feeling in the pit of my stomach.

"So," she says, "guess what Janice did."

"Got sick."

"All over the bathroom," she says.

"She deserves it," I say.

"For what?" Toby asks me.

"On general principles," I tell her.

"Are you mad at her for something?" she asks.

I am of course, because if it weren't for Janice, Dwyer wouldn't have had anybody to blackmail Marlene with. But I don't want to tell that to Toby. So I say, "No. I'm not mad at her. I just hope she wakes up before she turns into an alcoholic, that's all."

Toby laughs.

"She doesn't drink that much," she says. "She can't."

"You don't have to," I tell her.

"Well," she says. "She was pretty shook up."

"I can imagine," I say.

"It killed the party," she says.

"I bet."

"Did you run into Marlene last night?" she asks me. "Was she at Charlie's? With Dwyer?"

It's pretty obvious that Toby hasn't talked with Marlene, otherwise she would have said something by now, and she wouldn't be peppering me with questions, as if she were a reporter for *The Waterford Enquirer*.

"No," I tell her, "I didn't run into her." And then, before she can ask me anything else, I say,

"But listen, Toby, I'd like to talk more, but I've really got to get to work."

"Oh," she says. "Yeah. Okay. I guess I'll see you at school then."

"Right," I say. "But I've got to run. Okay?"

"Okay," she says.

I say, "G'bye."

She says, "G'day."

And I hang up the phone.

For a second, I just sit there looking at the phone and wondering if I should call Marlene. I figure, whatever happened last night, she's still my best friend, and she could probably use somebody to talk to.

But if she *did*—if she let Dwyer—then she's probably ashamed or at least embarrassed and, after everything I said to her last night, I'd probably be the last person in the world that she'd want to talk to.

And if, on the other hand, she *didn't*—let Dwyer—then she probably would have called to tell me by now, which she obviously hasn't.

So, I conclude, all things considered, maybe the best thing for me to do right now is just leave Marlene alone. Maybe that's what she needs—to be left alone. *And that way,* I tell myself, *at least the line will be free for Gary, in case he wants to call me.*

But he doesn't. I wait around as long as I can before I have to leave for work, but Gary doesn't call.

Which doesn't mean anything! That's what I tell myself, as I go out the door.

And as I hurry down the front walk, I tell myself, *It doesn't matter that he hasn't called. And even if*

121

it does break my heart a little, that only proves what I already knew.

There's no doubt about it, I tell myself, as I race for the bus stop, *I'm in love!*

Twenty-two

When I get done with work that night, I'm kind of hoping that I'll find Gary waiting for me in the lobby. But I don't.

I don't find him waiting for me outside the theatre either.

And I don't find him waiting for me in my secret garden behind the library.

But when I finally get home at around ten o'clock and walk into the kitchen, there's one of those little pink *While You Were Out* slips that my mother brings home from the office, pinned up on the bulletin board that we have by the phone.

As I walk over to the bulletin board, I tell myself not to get excited. *It could be Marlene,* I remind myself. *Or Toby. Or anybody.*

But my hand is practically shaking as I take the pink slip down from the bulletin board and—All right!—where it says, *Caller,* my mother has written—*Gary.* Where it says *Time,* she's written—*12:50.*

"Ee*haw!!*"

I let go with a rebel yell that caroms off the walls and echos all around the house.

"Angelica?"

Whoops! My mother's home.

"Hi!" I shout.

"Are you okay?" she calls to me.

She's upstairs in her room again.

"Yes," I call to her.

"Did you see your message?"

"Yes."

"He called right after you left."

"Great!" I say.

I look at the little pink slip in my hand—at the place where it says, *Caller's number.* It's blank.

"Did he leave his number?" I shout to my mother.

"No," she shouts.

I look at the phone, hanging on the wall, and then at the phone book, sitting on the counter.

Should I call him? If he wanted me to call him, wouldn't he have left his number?

Not necessarily. He might not have been home when he called. He might have been in a phone booth or at a friend's house.

But he's probably home by now.

I open the phone book and turn to the "E's."

Everson, Raymond rl est Wfd Vlg Est 724-1948

I lift the phone to my ear and get the dial tone.

I dial 724-1948.

I hear the phone ringing at the other end of the line. And then, after a couple of rings, somebody picks it up and a woman's voice says, "The number you are dialing, 724-1948 has been disconnected . . . The number you are dialing, 724-1948 has been disconnected."

"Are you coming up?" my mother shouts.

I hang up the phone.

"Angelica?"

I stand there, staring at the phone and wondering why Gary's phone has been disconnected.

"Yes," I shout. "In a minute."

Twenty-three

"Aren't you going to ask me?"

It's Monday morning and Marlene is driving me to school. Toby's not with us this morning. It's just the two of us.

"No," I tell her.

"I didn't," she says.

She's lying. I can tell by the look in her eyes, when she looks over at me.

"I didn't ask you," I tell her.

"But you wanted to know," she says.

"You're my best friend," I tell her.

"Well," she says, "I didn't."

"Great."

"You heard about Janice?" she asks me.

"Yes," I say. "Toby told me."

"Me, too," she says. "Dwyer's not going out with her anymore."

"Great."

"I asked him not to," she says. "And he promised he wouldn't."

"That's nice of him."

"He's nice!" she says.

"I believe you."

"He *is!*" she insists.

I nod and say, "Great."

Twenty-four

No Gary.

Usually, I pass him in the corridor between classes at least once or twice before lunchtime. But not this morning. I don't pass him in the corridor, and when I go to lunch I don't see him in the cafeteria.

I don't see Marlene either. She isn't sitting at our regular table with Janice and Gayle and Toby. *Maybe she's avoiding Janice,* I think. *Maybe I should too.*

But since I don't see Marlene sitting anywhere else in the cafeteria, I head for the people who are most likely to know where she is. As I sit down with Janice and Gayle and Toby at our regular table, I ask them, "What happened to Marlene?"

Gayle shrugs.

"Oh," she says, "she's probably just over at the mall."

Janice doesn't say anything.

But Toby looks around the cafeteria and says, "I don't see Dwyer either."

Gayle shoots Toby a look.

"So what?" she says.

Janice doesn't say anything.

I look down at my plate and say, "Meat loaf, again. God! Do I hate meat loaf!"

Janice says, "He's a shit."

Everyone looks at her.

She's got tears in her eyes.

"I always thought so," I tell her.

"What do *you* know about it?" she asks me.

"A lot more than you think," I tell her.

"Like what?" Toby asks me.

"Like none of your business," I tell her.

She looks hurt.

"Well," she says, "if *that's* the way you want to be!"

"I just don't think Dwyer's worth crying over," I tell her.

"Oh," says Janice, "and I suppose Gary Everson is!"

"Who said anything about Gary Everson?" I ask her.

"Everybody!" she says.

"What do you mean?" I ask her.

"Well," says Gayle, "what do you expect?"

"As long as he's been here," says Janice, "he's never gone out with anybody."

"Except me," I remind her.

"*Before* you," says Toby.

"That's almost a whole year," says Gayle.

"So?" I ask her.

"So," says Toby, "doesn't that tell you anything?"

"No," I say. "Not much."

"It doesn't tell you he's a *fag?*" asks Janice.

I just look at her.

Toby turns to me and says, "Unless, of course, you know better!"

I look at her.

"Angelica?" says Janice. "Ha!"

That does it!

I mean, I'm so angry at Janice anyway for sneaking around with Dwyer behind Marlene's back that I'd like to throw something—something hard and sharp—at her. But since I'm too civilized for that, I just look her in the eye and snarl, "What's *that* supposed to mean?"

And she snaps back, "What do you *think* it means?"

"What it *means*," I tell her, "is that it will take somebody a hell of a lot better than *Dwyer!*"

"Not according to Dwyer," she says.

I just look at her.

"He says that night, after Gayle's party, when he drove you home, you were all over him."

"What?!"

"But he wasn't interested," she says.

Which is so ridiculous, I have to laugh.

"That doesn't sound like Dwyer to *me!*" I say.

"Really?" says Janice.

"Really!" I tell her. "I mean, if you think about it, Dwyer's the kind of guy who'll take anything he can get *and the easier the better!*"

"He said he *loved* me!" Janice says and, bursting into tears, she jumps up from the table.

And Gayle looks at me and says, "Jesus, Angelica!" and, jumping up from the table, she puts her arm around Janice's shoulder and walks her out of the cafeteria.

Everybody stares at them. And everybody stares at me. And I feel lousy because, even if she was asking for it, which she was, I still hate to see Janice crying.

"Are you done?" asks Toby.

I look over at her and see her eyeing my meat loaf.

"Be my guest," I tell her and, shoving my tray over to her, I get up from the table and head for the door.

Twenty-five

I've still got a few minutes until the end of lunch hour, so I head for the bank of telephones down by the gym.

Luckily, when I get there, one of the phones is free. So I screw up my courage, pop my quarter in the slot, and dial Gary's number.

And there's my old friend—"The number you are dialing, 724-1948, has been disconnected."

I hang up the phone. Now, I'm really starting to worry.

I mean, first, Gary's phone gets disconnected, and then, he doesn't show up for school.

Something's wrong. But what?

Has Gary been kidnapped by the CIA? Has he been abducted by aliens? Maybe he never existed at all. Maybe he was just a figment of my imagination, like a movie star that you fall in love with and then never see again. Like James Dean.

God! Maybe he's dead! God! I can just see myself, visiting his grave—a widow, dressed in black, wearing a veil and carrying a single red rose. I can see his gravestone—

EVERSON, GARY
1970–1987
"To know, know, know him
Is to love, love, love him . . ."

131

Just thinking about it, I'm almost in tears. In fact, I'd probably break down and start crying right there, if just then a bunch of guys hadn't come barging out of the gym.

But when I see these guys walking toward me, and I realize that they're all on the tennis team, and I spot Brian Avery among them, I pull myself together.

When they're opposite me and just about to walk by me, I say, "Brian? Can I talk to you for a minute?"

The whole gang stops right in front of me, and everybody looks at Brian, and Brian looks at me— like he doesn't recognize me, like he's never seen me before in his life.

So I remind him.

"Angelica," I tell him.

But Brian just keeps looking at me until after a second one of his friends says, "Sorry Angelica, but Bry's not signing any autographs today."

And everybody laughs.

But Brian just keeps looking at me.

"Yeah?" he says.

"Have you seen Gary?" I ask him.

"Gary?" he says, like he doesn't know who I'm talking about.

"Everson," I tell him.

He looks at me like, *Why am I asking him?*

But then, he shakes his head and says, "No. Not that I remember."

And then, turning to the guys he's with, he says, "Have you seen Everson?"

They all shrug and shake their heads.

Turning back to me, Brian shrugs and says, "Sorry."

The class bell rings.

I say, "Thanks."

Brian says, "Sure."

I turn and take off down the corridor. But before I'm out of earshot, I hear one of Brian's pals say, "Pretty young, Bry!"

And then I hear *Bry* say, "Well, *young* anyway."

And everybody laughs.

Wonderful! You ask a guy a simple question, and what do you get?

Insulted.

Some way to treat a widow, huh?

Twenty-six

My first impression of the model home that Gary lives in has nothing to do with architecture or landscaping or anything like that. It has to do with the law—in the form of the police car that's parked in front of it.

I tell myself, *This could be worse than I imagined!* I mean, maybe Gary *has* been killed! Maybe burglars broke into his house, thinking everybody was out, but Gary was in bed with the twenty-four-hour flu and when he heard a noise and came downstairs to investigate, he walked in on the burglars and caught them red-handed, and they just turned around and shot him in cold blood, so there wouldn't be any witnesses!

That's crazy! I tell myself. *Things like that don't happen in Waterford!* But then, why is there a police car parked in front of Gary's house?

I knew this was a mistake. I mean, just because I happen to be in love with Gary, that doesn't give me a license to go dropping in on him, whenever I feel like it. Even if, when I tried to call him again after school, his phone was still disconnected.

That's when I got the idea to "drop by" Gary's house and see if he was home.

As soon as I got the idea, I rejected it. But then a funny thing happened when I got off the bus, the one that I took home from school because Marlene never came back from lunch and I didn't feel like walking home.

When I got to Eastern Boulevard, where you take a right turn to get to my house, my feet just kept on walking straight ahead until they brought me here. I mean, I tried to stop them, but they wouldn't listen to me.

So, here I am, standing on the street in front of Gary's house. Me and the police car.

So? I ask my feet. *What do we do now?*

While they're thinking it over, I look around me at what I can see of Waterford Village Estates.

Actually, there isn't that much to see yet. So far, Waterford Village Estates still looks pretty much like the open field that it was before Gary's father bought it, except now the field is crisscrossed with a network of unpaved streets and a sprinkling of fire hydrants, and here and there you can see three or four houses in various stages of construction.

But that's about it, except for Gary's house which, being the model home for the whole development, is finished and landscaped and—now that I look at it—really beautiful.

It's a modern house, but not *too* modern. Made of fieldstone and glass and trimmed with cedar and cedar shingles, it's built all on one floor and sits up on a little rise, looking down over a freshly-sodded lawn. It's a model home with a model young man waiting inside—waiting for me to do something.

So what am I waiting for?

Nothing.

Okay, feets, do your stuff!

I kick my Reeboks into gear and set out for Gary's front door.

I march past the police car, up Gary's driveway,

and over the little flagstone walk that runs from the driveway to the front landing.

I climb the front steps to the landing and reach the front door and ring the bell.

I hear the doorbell chiming inside the house.

I wait.

The door opens.

Officer Glenn Van Dyke looks out at me and says, "What do you want?"

I freeze.

For a second, I'm so scared by the way Van Dyke looks—and the way he's looking at me—that I seriously consider saying, *Oh, excuse me. I must have the wrong model home.*

But I'm too worried about what's happened to Gary to back down now. So, after a second, I swallow hard and say, "Is Gary here?"

"Who's that?"

It's Gary, calling from inside the house, and he sounds okay. I heave a sigh of relief and call into the house, "It's me! Angelica!"

"Angelica what?" says Van Dyke.

I want to tell him, *None of your business!* but the way he's looking at me, I'm afraid he'll pull out his gun and point it at me and say, *Spread 'em!*

So I tell him, "Pierce."

"Hi," says Gary.

I can see him inside the house, peeking out at me from over Van Dyke's shoulder.

"Are you okay?" I ask him.

"Yeah," he says.

But he doesn't look it. He looks nervous and upset.

"Your mother's Peggy Pierce?" Van Dyke asks me. "Works for David Manion?"

I tell him, "Yes." And then, before he can ask

136

me another question, I look over his shoulder at Gary and say, "I tried to call you."

"Oh," he says. "I should have told you."

"You don't look like her," says Van Dyke.

I want to say, *No shit?* but I don't. I say, "So?"

Van Dyke narrows his eyes at me and says, "Does she know you're here?"

"Yes," I lie.

But he doesn't believe me. I can tell by the way he screws his face up in a smirk and nods his head.

I'm thinking, *What if he decides to check on me and finds out that I'm lying?*

But Gary says, "Is that all, officer?"

And Van Dyke turns to him and says, "Yeah. For now."

"Great," says Gary.

"You just be sure and tell your father I'm looking for him," Van Dyke tells him.

"I'll tell him," says Gary.

Van Dyke nods and turns back to me. But before he can say anything or ask me any more questions, Gary peeks over his shoulder at me and says, "Are you coming in?"

Which is a problem because I'm not really sure that I want to, or that Gary wants me to, or if he's just being polite, or if he's just trying to get rid of Van Dyke, or what.

But with Van Dyke standing there studying me, I decide to go with the answer that seems the most natural under the circumstances. So as if I'd been planning on coming in all along, I tell Gary, "Yeah," and I look up at Van Dyke, who's blocking the doorway.

Van Dyke looks down at me.

I say, "Excuse me," meaning, *Get out of my way.*

But Van Dyke doesn't move. He just looks at me and then, after a second, instead of stepping out onto the landing or stepping back inside the house, he just turns in the doorway, so that there's just enough room between him and the door frame for me to squeeze past him—which I'm not about to do.

I just stand there, looking at him and waiting for him to figure it out.

And I guess he does because, after a second, he smiles at me and then, turning to Gary, he says, "I'll be back."

Gary says, "I'll tell him."

Van Dyke nods and says, "Have a good day."

Just like that.

And then, turning to me, he tips his hat and says, "Ma'am."

And then, stepping out onto the landing, he brushes past me and thumps off down the steps.

For a second, I just stand there watching him swaggering off toward his car.

But then Gary has my hand and, pulling me into the house and closing the door behind me, he kisses me—too hard, too hungrily.

And then, breaking it off too quickly, he says, "What are you doing here?"

Stunned and angry, I say, "You sound like *him!*" meaning Van Dyke and nodding toward the door.

Embarrassed and contrite, Gary nods and takes me in his arms and holds me close and whispers, "I'm sorry."

I sigh and say, "It's okay."

"I'm . . ." he says. But he doesn't finish.

He lets me go and turns away from me and looks down at the floor and shakes his head.

I guess he's really upset about Van Dyke—about Van Dyke's coming here, looking for his father.

"What's he want with . . . ?" I start to ask Gary about his father, but as I do, I suddenly notice something weird—the house is empty!

I mean, from where I'm standing in the front hallway, I can't see a single piece of furniture. Not a table or a chair. Not a painting on the wall. Not a mirror. Not a curtain on a window. Nothing!

I look at Gary.

He's looking at me.

"What happened?" I ask him.

He shakes his head and says, "Let's go into the living room."

I take his hand and follow where he leads me—down the hall and into the living room. It's a beautiful room with a high ceiling and a huge fireplace that faces a big bay window with a beautiful, upholstered leather window seat.

But like the front hallway, it's bare. Or almost bare. Gathered like an island in the middle of the room is a mattress, an orange crate, an ice chest, a hot plate, a cassette player/recorder, an alarm clock, some books and papers, and a guitar.

"What's going on?" I ask Gary.

"Have a seat," he says, motioning to the mattress.

I sit down.

He sits down next to me.

He looks so unhappy. I reach out and take his hand and say, "You don't have to tell me."

"No," he says. "I have to."

"Is it bad?" I ask.

He laughs and shakes his head and says, "It ain't good!"

"Your father?" I ask him.

He sighs and says, "Yeah. But it's not him, really. It's everybody he was depending on."

"Oh," I say.

"Everything's been repossessed," he says. "The furniture, the appliances. Everything but the car—which is paid for—and this—" he gestures to the stuff around us. "Which is mine," he says.

"The guitar?" I ask him.

He shakes his head.

"No," he says. "I borrowed that from Alan."

"Oh," I say. "I thought you didn't play."

He smiles at me.

"I don't," he says. "You should hear me."

As if he were actually offering to play for me, I say, "Okay."

He laughs.

"How bad is it?" I ask him.

"My guitar playing," he asks me, "or my life?"

"Either," I say.

"My guitar playing's the worst, and my life . . ."

He shakes his head.

"I'm okay," he says. "But my father's in trouble. At least, Waterford Village Estates is. But they're the same thing."

He sighs.

"It's a long story," he says. "Interest rates shot up. Sales slowed down. One of my father's partners backed out on him . . ."

"And your mother," I add.

He nods.

"Yeah," he says. "As soon as things started to go bad."

I look at him.

"It wasn't just that she didn't like it here," he says. "She didn't. But that wasn't it. It was seeing my father's dream going down the drain. It was his

140

dream that was dying, but she couldn't take it. So, she just . . .''

He doesn't finish. He can't. He's got tears in his eyes.

"Oh, Gary!"

I put my arms around him.

"Don't!" he says. And he pulls away from me.

"I'm sorry . . ."

"No," he says. "*I* am. I just . . . You don't know him," he says, "my father. He's a genius. I mean, he can make something out of nothing. That's what he *does*.

"He took a storefront in Queens and turned it into a string of aerobic dance studios that spread into Manhattan and over into New Jersey. He took a beat-up old restaurant in Cape Cod and turned it into a first class dinner theatre. And—God!—a million other things like that.

"And this place! This is the biggest and best thing he ever dreamed up. A whole community! For people to live in and raise their families.

"You should see the plans," he says. "It was going to be *beautiful!* But now . . ." He shakes his head.

"My father's out there, flying all around the country, trying to raise money. And to get it—if he *can* get it—he'll probably have to sell off most of his interest in this place.

"But he'll do it, if he has to," he says, "if that's what it takes to make it happen.

"He won't quit," he says. "And I won't quit on him. I'm all he's got."

"Then he's got a lot," I say.

Gary looks over at me.

"You really think so?" he says.

I nod.

He smiles.

"You're a good friend," he says.

"Is that all?" I ask him.

He shakes his head and looks into my eyes and says, "Just the beginning."

And it suddenly occurs to me that we're practically in bed together!

I mean, if there *were* a bed under the mattress that we're sitting on, we'd be in it!

It's a pretty scary thought, too scary to dwell on. So I say, "What about Van Dyke? What's he got to do with it?"

Gary shrugs.

"Oh," he says, "we owe a lot of people money. And some of them have gone to court and gotten judgments against us."

"Oh," I say.

"It's nothing we can't straighten out if my father can come up with some fresh money," he says. "But meanwhile, Van Dyke keeps coming around, looking for him, asking me when he'll be back . . ."

"What do you tell him?"

Gary smiles.

"I tell him that I expect him back any day now."

"Do you?"

Gary shakes his head.

"I don't know," he says. "If he can't come up with anything . . ."

He shrugs.

"Where is he now?"

Gary laughs.

"Now *you* sound like him," he says, meaning Van Dyke and nodding toward the door.

"I just wondered," I tell him.

"Las Vegas," he says.

"Gambling?"

Gary laughs.

"I guess you could call it that," he says. "Except he's doing it in a bank instead of a casino."

"Well," I say, "I guess that makes the odds better."

"Yeah," says Gary. "But either way, the house always wins."

"Well," I say, "maybe not this time."

Gary looks at me, looks into my eyes, and says, "I'm sorry about before."

He's talking about when he kissed me before—about how rough he was.

"That's okay," I tell him.

"I guess I was . . ."

He shrugs.

"I don't know," he says. "Scared, I guess."

"I guess I would be, too," I tell him.

"I just needed . . ."

He shakes his head.

"To be loved," I say.

He looks at me.

"Yeah," he says.

"I know," I say.

"You do?"

"Yes."

"So?" he says. "It's okay? Are you sure?"

I nod.

And he smiles.

And he kisses me again, but sweetly this time to chase away the bitter taste of our last kiss.

And then, he says, "Better?"

"Much," I say.

"Ready for dinner?" he says.

Which cracks me up.

But it turns out that he isn't kidding. He's really inviting me to dinner. Here.

And not only that, he intends to *cook* dinner for us. Here. On his hot plate.

He shows me the pot that he intends to cook dinner in and then, opening his ice chest—which contains no ice and which he calls his pantry—he takes out a box of macaroni and cheese dinner, stick of margarine, and a can of condensed milk.

"Pasta a la Kraft," he says.

And a bottle of wine.

"Ruffino Chianti, Riserva Ducale, 1978."

"Where'd you get that?" I ask him.

He smiles and says, "I'll show you."

He takes my hand and helps me to my feet and leads me out into the hallway.

About halfway down the hall, he stops by a door and nods to it and says, "The wine cellar."

And then he opens the door on a closet—a big closet—that's filled from the floor to the ceiling with rows and rows of wine bottles. "I've got to drink all of them," he tells me, "before the liquor store repossesses them."

I look at him to see if he's serious.

He isn't.

"Well," I say, "if I'm really your friend, I guess I ought to help you out."

Gary smiles.

"If it's okay with my mother," I add.

It won't be, I know it. I know, if I tell my mother that I'm in this big empty house, and I'm planning to stay for dinner with Mr. Smoothie, she'll probably think I'm planning to stay for breakfast too.

I mean, there's no way she'd put up with it. If she knew.

So I'll have to tell her something else. Like a lie.

Like I could tell her that I'm having dinner with Marlene, so we can study together after dinner for a big test or something, which—because it's something I've done before—she'd probably believe.

"Can I use your phone?" I ask Gary.

I've forgotten about his phone's being disconnected, but suddenly remembering, I say, "Oh! Your phone!"

Gary laughs.

"I meant to tell you," he says. "Our personal phone has been disconnected, but if you call 724-1949 and you hear a voice saying, 'Waterford Village Estates. May I help you?' that's me, answering the phone that *hasn't* been disconnected.

"Waterford Village Estates is still in business," he says. "It's just the Everson family that's defunct."

He says it like a joke, but he isn't laughing.

"Come on," he says, and he leads me down the hall to another empty room that used to be his father's office.

The telephone is sitting on the floor. Gary picks it up and, as he hands it to me, he says, "Are you hungry? I can get started."

"I think you'd better wait," I tell him.

He shakes his head.

"I always plan on things working out," he says.

"I don't know . . ." I start to say, but Gary's already out the door and gone.

So, I take a deep breath and lift the receiver and dial my number. But no one answers.

My mother isn't home yet. She's probably still at the office.

I call her there, and she answers, and I say, "Hi, Mom." And right away, before I can tell her about

Marlene and dinner and the big test we have to study for and everything, my mother tells me that she's been trying to reach me for the last hour because something's come up at the office, and she's going to have to work late tonight.

You'd think that would be a big relief, but it isn't, because I don't believe her, and it really ticks me off because I was beginning to think she'd quit "working late" with David Manion.

But nonetheless, as angry as it makes me, I tell myself, *This is just the break I needed,* and all I say is, "How late do you think you'll be?"

"I don't know," she says. "But don't wait up for me."

I feel like saying, *Don't you wait up for me!* but I just say, "I won't."

"I think there's still some stew left in the refrigerator," she says.

"Don't worry about it," I tell her. "I'll find something to eat."

"Okay," she says. "I'm sorry."

"No problem," I tell her.

She says, "Thanks, Angel."

I say, "Have a good time."

She says, "I don't think so."

"No," I say. "I guess not."

Twenty-seven

Gary's pasta a la Kraft isn't half bad, and the wine—the Ruffino Chianti whatever—is really good. But I'm not overdoing it.

I've only had one glass. Half a glass. So it isn't the wine that's got me feeling this way. It's Gary—how nice he is and how sweet he's being, telling me the story of his life, his impressions of Waterford, his plans for conquering the world, goofing on all of it, telling jokes on himself, turning on the charm and watching me lap it all up.

Which I do, I admit. I mean, what can I say? The guy's got it! And I want all of it that I can get!

So, after dinner, when we're in the kitchen and just about finished cleaning up, I reach for the part that Gary's been holding back.

"Is it almost time for the entertainment?" I ask him.

He smiles and says, "What did you have in mind?"

I can see, by the look in his eye, what *he* has in mind, but I say, "Music."

And he looks at me like he doesn't know what I'm talking about.

"Something original," I suggest. "Something live."

For a second, Gary just grins at me, but then he nods and says, "Okay."

"Really?" I say.

I can't believe it!

But Gary tells me that he's finally written a song that "isn't that bad." "Actually," he says, "it sounds pretty good. At least, in my head."

He laughs.

"The problem is how bad it sounds when I try *singing* it," he says. "But I've got the answer to that too."

"You're going to get a voice transplant?" I guess.

He laughs and shakes his head and, as he reaches for his wallet, he says, "Do you smoke?"

I look at him.

"Cigarettes?" I ask him.

He shakes his head and then, opening his wallet and reaching into it, he takes out a hand-rolled cigarette—a joint.

I can't say that I'm shocked. I mean, it's not the first time that I've seen one.

The first time was at Gayle's Halloween party— the one that Dwyer drove me home from, the one where he tried to make a move on me and I told him where to go.

That night, Dwyer—who else?—brought a couple of joints to the party and quite a few kids tried smoking them.

I kind of hung back. Not because I was afraid, exactly. I mean, I didn't think if I took one puff the devil would pop up and steal my soul or anything. But suppose I liked it? I mean, what do I need another bad habit for? To wreck my lungs? To empty my pockets? To wrap me up in a haze, like Alan Sinclair?

No thanks.

Which is what I said to Marlene when she walked over and offered me the joint she was smoking.

I'd pretty much decided against it. But by then, almost everybody else at the party had tried it. And they were all so proud of themselves for being so brave and everything that they really got on me.

So, since I didn't really think it was such a big deal—I mean, nobody who'd tried it had been struck by lightning or anything—and because I was curious, I told myself, *What the heck!* and took the joint from Marlene.

Everybody cheered as I lifted the joint to my lips and took a puff. But a second later, when I started coughing my lungs out, everybody laughed.

So that was it, my one and only dope-smoking experience—one puff, which I didn't get the least bit high from. All I got was a little embarrassed.

But that was the last time I ran across it— marijuana, I mean—although I've heard that quite a few seniors smoke it quite a lot.

I've heard, if you go to a party where there are a lot of seniors around, sooner or later before the night is over, somebody or other will probably pull out a joint and light it up and start passing it around.

But still, if I'm not exactly shocked by Gary's having a joint, I *am* surprised.

"Did you have that on you all the time?" I ask him. "When Van Dyke was here?"

Gary smiles.

"Van Dyke's dumb," he says, "but he's not so dumb that he'd go searching for my father in my wallet."

"No," I say. "I guess not, but . . . where'd you get it?"

"From a friend," he says.

Probably Alan Sinclair, I think. But I don't ask.

"So?" he says. "Do you? Smoke?"

"I have," I tell him.

"And . . . ?" he says.

I shrug, like it was no big deal, which it wasn't.

"Well, you don't have to if you don't feel like it," he says. "And I won't if you don't want me to. Except—to be honest with you—I can't stand to hear myself singing when I'm straight.

"But after a couple of tokes of this . . ."

He pretends to take a puff of the joint. And then, as if he were stoned, he says, "Say, who is this guy who calls himself Sting, anyway?"

I laugh.

And Gary does too.

And then he says, "Come on. We're done in here. It's time to go into the studio."

And he takes my hand and leads me out of the kitchen and down the hallway.

Back in the living room, he leads me right past his guitar and over to the mattress, where he sits down beside me and takes a pack of matches out of his pocket and lights up the joint. And—God!—the smell! I'd almost forgotten.

In case you've never smelled marijuana burning, what it smells like is a skunkweed cigar. But the smell doesn't seem to bother Gary, so I pretend that it doesn't bother me.

While Gary smokes, I just sit there, breathing through my mouth and wondering what I'm going to do when Gary offers the joint to me, which—after taking a toke or two—he does.

"Do yourself a favor," he says.

I look at the joint, and then I look at Gary.

"Your singing can't be *that* bad," I tell him.

"I warn you," he says, "if you're straight when I start singing . . ." He shakes his head.

"I can't be responsible," he says.

I laugh.

I tell myself, *You don't really want to do this!* And I keep laughing.

But on the other hand, I tell myself, *you don't want to be a drag either!* And I heave a sigh.

"Well," I say, "I guess one puff won't hurt."

Gary smiles.

"It'll help," he says. And he passes me the joint.

I take it, and I look at it, and then I look over at Gary and say, "You promise me, you won't laugh if I start coughing?"

Gary grins and says, "I promise."

And I nod, as if that were all the assurance that I needed, and I say, "Okay," and I bring the joint up to my lips, and I take a little puff, and I pull it down into my lungs, and I hold it there for a second, and then I let it go.

"Very good!" says Gary, like he's really impressed.

I shrug and say, "Nothing to it," and I take another little puff. And I start coughing.

And Gary starts laughing.

"Hey!" I remind him, as soon as I can catch my breath, "You promised!"

Choking off his laughter, Gary says, "Sorry."

I pass the joint back to him.

As he takes it, I say, "Do you smoke a lot?"

He shakes his head.

"No," he says, and he takes another toke, and while he's holding down the smoke, he says, "only on special occasions."

"Like making your debut as a rock star?" I ask him.

151

Exhaling the smoke, Gary smiles and shakes his head and says, "Like just being here with you."

And he kisses me, and it's the best kiss ever.

It says, "I love you," and it says, "I want you."

Both at once and neither more than the other.

And when it's over and Gary leans back away from me and looks into my eyes, his eyes say the same thing.

"I think you'd better sing," I tell him.

He smiles and says, "Are you sure you wouldn't rather . . . ?"

"No," I tell him, "I'm not. Which is why you'd better sing."

He grins and says, "Okay. You asked for it!" and with that, he gets up from the mattress and walks over to his guitar.

It's sitting on the floor across from us. He squats down next to it and lifts it into his lap. Then, as he rocks back onto his heels and begins tuning it up, he says, "Alan gave me this tune about a month ago. More. Maybe six weeks ago. But I couldn't find the words for it.

"It's such a pretty thing," he says. "I didn't want to slap just anything on it, you know? I wanted to find the words that were meant for it."

Still tuning his guitar, he gets to his feet and walks back to me.

"But I couldn't find them," he says. "Until the night I bumped into you—in the garden, behind the library."

I look him in the eye and cock my head and say, "My mother's right about you."

And Gary laughs.

But then he stops laughing and looks me in the eye and says, "It happens to be true."

Which is kind of thrilling, when you think about it. I mean, if it's really true.

Because—imagine—actually *inspiring* somebody to write a song! I mean, what could be better?

"I got the idea for it that night," he says. "And the first words the day after that. And the rest of it's been coming in dribs and drabs ever since. I just finished it this afternoon."

"Is that why you weren't in school?" I ask him.

He nods and says, "First things first."

"You cut school to finish the song?"

He nods and says, "I started working on it this morning, and I was so close to finishing it I couldn't put it down. It wouldn't let me."

"And it's really about *me?*" I ask him.

Gary smiles and, as if he didn't want to admit it, he says, "Well, it's about this beautiful woman and this kind of lonely guy and what happens when they meet.

"But," he says, shrugging it off, as if it were just a coincidence, "any resemblance between the characters portrayed in the song and real people is strictly intentional."

Which cracks me up and also blows me away because, unless I'm wrong, Gary is actually telling me that he *was* thinking of me when he wrote the song that he's about to play.

"Ready?" he says.

"I can't wait!" I tell him.

Gary nods and takes a deep breath and lets it out with a sigh.

"Okay," he says. "Here goes."

He settles down to the floor in front of me and rests his guitar in his lap. He glances over at me and looks down at his guitar. And then, he begins to play.

He starts out very slowly, picking out each note, one by one, so that his playing sounds kind of wooden and mechanical—like an old music box, slowly returning to life after years of neglect.

But then, as the figure he's playing begins repeating itself, he settles into a gently rolling rhythm and, as he does, the notes begin blending together in perfect waves of sweet and lulling sound.

I close my eyes and let the sound wash over me. My breathing falls into tempo with the music's flow. My mood shifts into phase with its bittersweet feeling.

And then, as Gary begins singing, my heart fills with a feeling beyond happiness and, behind my closed eyelids, my eyes fill with tears.

In a voice, neither pretty nor rough, but somehow both at once, with all the feeling of someone who's seen a lot but hasn't stopped believing, Gary sings . . .

"And she said, 'Call me Susan.
'Cause it's Tuesday and I hope we'll be friends.
I'll be Susan just for you.
Then I never will be Susan again.'
  Hello, Sue!
  How are you?
  I am, too.
    La-da-da
    La-da-da
    La-da-da

'Night's ahead,' said Miss Susan.
'Couldn't you stay here and help me pretend?
'I'll be Susan all night through.
'Then I never will be Susan again.'

Love ya', Sue.
Love ya' true.
Yes, I do.
 La-da-da
 La-da-da
 La-da-da

Time to wonder in the morning,
When Miss Susan's done and gone.
Now we're holding back the dawn
And holding on.
And holding on.
 La-da-da
 La-da-da
 La-da-da.
  La-da-da
  La da-da
  La-da-da

Then I said, 'Mornin','
Feeling feelings that I didn't intend.
Feeling, Stay and see it through.
Whatcha' got to lose in the end?
 La-da-da
 La-da-da
 La-da-da
  La-da-da
  La-da-da
  La-da-da
And she said, 'Call me Susan.' ''

As the last notes of the song echo and fade, I open my eyes.

Gary's looking at me.

"Well?" he says.

"That's really her name?" I ask him. "The girl in the song? Susan?"

155

Gary smiles and says, "Maybe."

"You don't know?" I ask him. "Or you won't say?"

Gary nods and says, "Yup."

"It's a secret?"

"A mystery," he says.

"Oh."

"Like you," he says.

"Me?"

He nods and says, "What do you think of it?"

"The song?" I ask him.

He laughs.

"Not the singer," he says.

Through the tears welling in my eyes, I look into his eyes, and I tell him, "It's very beautiful."

I can see that he's pleased, but he's embarrassed too. Smiling and blushing at the same time—and shrugging off my compliment as if it were only flattery—he says, "Well . . ."

"No!" I tell him. "I mean it! It's one of the saddest and happiest and prettiest—"

"Now, wait a minute!" He laughs.

"Really!" I insist. "Oh, Gary! You're really good! You *could* be a star!"

"With my voice?" he says. "How much of that stuff did you smoke?"

"Not enough to make me crazy," I tell him. "I mean it. I mean, your voice isn't pretty—"

"I'll say!"

"But it's real," I say. "I mean, I can feel what you're feeling—what you're really feeling—as you sing. And that makes the story that you're telling seem true.

"I mean, I can *see* the people you're singing about. I can imagine how they look and what

156

they're doing and what they're feeling. Everything!"

"Really?" he says.

"Yes!" I tell him.

"Maybe you should make a video of it," he says.

I laugh, although I have to admit that as I was talking the idea did cross my mind.

I wonder if Gary knew? I wonder if he knows? Even though I've never told him about my dream of making movies, it would be just like him to know.

"Seriously," he says. "You should."

"I *could*," I tell him, "if I knew how."

He shrugs and says, "Join the video club."

I shake my head and tell him, "No."

"Why not?" he says.

He *is* serious.

"I don't know," I say.

"We could be stars together," he says.

I look at him.

"Why not?" he says.

"You really think I could, don't you?"

"If I can write a song," he says, "and sing it and not have you holding your hands over your ears and running out of the room—Jesus, Angelica!—anything's possible!"

Which makes me laugh.

And Gary, too.

"I love your voice," I tell him.

"I love you," he says.

I look into his eyes.

"I love you, too," I tell him.

He smiles and says, "I guess we're in love."

"Yes," I say. "So, now what do we do?"

And he grins and says, "We make love."

I've never been so scared in my life. But I know he's right. There's nothing else to do, except—

"You don't have to worry," he says. "I'll take care of everything. I love you, Angelica."

So there's nothing else to do. And there's nothing else to say, except—

"Okay . . ."

Twenty-eight

They say it's never good the first time because you're so scared and he's so scared. But Gary wasn't scared at all and, although I was at first, once we started kissing, I got so caught up in loving him and his loving me—so swept up in the flood of sensations and emotions—that I lost track of my fears.

I lost track of the time too, I guess, because now, as Gary strikes a match and lights a candle and sets it up on his orange crate, I realize that it's grown dark.

From the mattress where I lie, I look up at him, kneeling beside me.

Naked in the candlelight, he looks so beautiful—so smooth-skinned, supple-muscled, long and lean—it's hard to believe that he's mine.

But while my body still tingles with the memory of his touch—he was so gentle with me, so patient, sweet and loving—I can hardly deny it.

And there's more proof in the smile he gives me as he catches me looking at him.

"What time is it?" I ask him.

Grinning, he looks down at me and says, "It isn't twelve, yet."

"It isn't Saturday night either," I tell him.

Still grinning, he lies down beside me and props

himself up on his elbow, so that his face is directly above me and his eyes are looking into mine.

"I want to make love to you, again," he says. "Again and again. All night long. And all day tomorrow. And . . ."

I smile and take his hand and rest it on my breast.

"Me, too," I say. "But if my mother gets home before I do, she's going to ground me for eternity."

Nodding, Gary reaches for his pants and reaches into his pocket and takes out his wristwatch. He looks at it and smiles at me and says, "It's not even nine-thirty."

Then, putting his watch back inside his pocket and tossing his pants aside, he leans back over me and says, "It's still early."

Which—in a way—I guess it is, considering that my mother told me not to wait up for her. But what if something came up at the last minute? What if, for example, as a surprise, Mrs. Manion suddenly decided she'd drive into town and drop by her husband's office and take him out for dinner?

Not that she would. But what if she did? Where would that leave my mother? Where would it leave me?

That's what I'm thinking as Gary bends down to kiss me, and why—even though I'd love for him to kiss me—I gather the sheet around me and roll away from him and jump up to my feet and say, "I've got to go."

"You look great in that," says Gary, admiring my sheet.

I blush and say, "Really. I've got to."

"I'll drive you home," he says.

I say, "Thank you," and bending down, I gather

up my clothes from the floor and scuffle off to the bathroom.

The moment I arrive, I close the door behind me and look into the mirror, where I see an incredibly happy young woman looking back at me and feel myself envying her, as I've never envied anyone else before.

Twenty-nine

When I get home, my mother's waiting for me. It's almost ten o'clock, and she's furious. She's been waiting for me since seven.

She's been "nearly frantic," she tells me. She even called Marlene's house, looking for me.

Struggling to control her temper, she looks me straight in the eye and demands to know where I've been all this time, and who I was with, and what I was doing.

As calmly as I can, I tell her where I've been (in case Van Dyke actually checked up on me) and who I was with (in case she saw Gary pulling his car up in front of the house). But do I tell her what I was doing?

Do you think I'm crazy?

No, I tell her that Gary and I have been studying together for a big test.

But she doesn't believe me because—as she always does whenever I'm out of her sight for more than five minutes—she just naturally assumes that I've been up to something slutty.

Which I haven't, I tell myself. *Even if she has! Or has she?* I wonder.

"I thought you were working late," I tell her.

"The other side agreed to settle," she explains.

"Oh."

"If they hadn't," she says, "I'd have been up half the night, getting ready for court tomorrow."

"Well *I* didn't know that," I tell her. "So when Mrs. Everson asked me if I'd stay to dinner, I said yes."

I hold my breath.

She buys it. She buys it, but she doesn't like it.

"You should have called me!" she insists.

"I didn't see any point," I explain, "with you so busy and everything."

"The point is" she says, "I'm your *mother!* And I need to know where you *are!*"

I heave a sigh and make a grab for the nearest silver lining.

"Well," I say, "I'm here now."

"Yes," she says. "And here is where you'll stay."

"No!"

"Yes!" she says. "Every night for the next two weeks."

"Two weeks?!"

"There will be no going out with boys—Gary or anybody else—and no staying over with friends and nobody dropping in to visit. You're grounded!"

"But, Mom, I only—"

"I won't have you running wild all over town without anybody knowing where you are or what you're up to. I'm responsible for you. And since you can't be trusted to behave responsibly when you're out," she says, "I want you home, alone, every night for the next two weeks."

"You can't!"

"Oh, *can't* I?"

I don't have to tell you the rest. I fought with her, long and loud. But it didn't do me any good.

Even crying didn't help. As always, in the end, my mother won.

So, I'm grounded. For *two weeks!* Can you imagine?

I mean, here I've just fallen in love—and *made* love—for the first time in my life. And here I am, in *love* with love and *making* love. And here *she* is—*Bang!* like a shot through my heart—locking me up in my house, away from the boy I love, night after night for *two whole weeks!*

I mean, if I'd told her the truth—if I'd told my mother that I'd spent the afternoon and evening making love to Gary Everson on a mattress in the middle of his living room floor—she couldn't have come up with a crueler punishment.

But still, there isn't much that I can do about it, is there? Other than acting like a model prisoner, in hopes that she'll relent and give me time off for good behavior.

That, and make the most of the daylight hours that she's left me.

So, before I fall asleep that night, that's what I decide to do.

Both.

Thirty

I don't give my mother a hard time, like she probably expects me to. I don't bitch about my punishment. I don't mope around the house. I don't whine or sulk.

Beginning the very next morning and through all the days that follow, I am a dream daughter, the Brownie Queen, the sweetest, most thoughtful, most considerate and cooperative little girl in the whole wide world.

It's enough to make you sick.

But at the same time, since Gary and I can't get together nights, we start getting together whenever we can.

Before school and between classes, at lunch hour and after school, whenever we get a chance, we get together and sneak off to out-of-the-way places where no one can see us or just duck around corners when no one's looking and throw ourselves into frenzies of hot necking and heavy petting.

But no matter how often we get together or how completely we surrender ourselves to each other when we do, it's never enough; and each time we part, I find myself already impatient for the next time.

In fact, in no time at all, "the next time" is all that I can think about.

Which—plus the fact that I'm spending all of my free time with Gary—doesn't make me too popular with my friends.

Toby's pissed at me. Gayle's bitchy. And Janice—who for some reason, after our scene in the cafeteria, decided that she wanted to be my friend and spend more time with me—is pissed *and* bitchy.

Only Marlene doesn't seem to care that I'm dedicating every moment of my waking life to Gary. The truth is, I'm not even sure that Marlene's noticed because she's been dedicating every moment of *her* waking life to Dwyer.

In fact, it's been over a week since I talked with Marlene, other than just saying, "Hi," or "How's it going?" or whatever, when I passed her in the halls.

The last time we had a conversation—if you could call it that—was a week ago last Tuesday morning, the day after my mother first grounded me, when Marlene caught up with me between classes and told me that she wouldn't be driving me to school anymore because from now on she'd be driving Dwyer.

And parking with him on the way to school, was what I guessed. But since it was her car and her life—and none of my business, really—I didn't say anything. All I said was, "I understand."

"I doubt it," said Marlene, sounding as snotty as I'd ever heard her and giving me this real patronizing smile, like all of a sudden she was a "real woman" and I was just a squirt.

I can't tell you how pissed I was. I mean, if it hadn't been for the fact that I didn't want Marlene or anybody else to know about Gary and me, I would have told her right on the spot that she didn't hold the patent on making love.

But I felt lousy too, because I suddenly realized that I'd lost my best friend. Marlene had made a choice. When she decided she couldn't live without Dwyer, she also decided that she'd have to get along without me. She didn't think her world was big enough to include both the boy she loved and the girlfriend who thought that the boy she loved was a bully and a jerk.

She was probably right too. As much as I liked Marlene, I could never pretend that I was happy about her being Dwyer's girl.

Even if I tried, as well as Marlene knew me, she'd see right through me.

I can't tell you how awful I felt or how sad it made me. But I felt angry too.

I wanted to tell Marlene how much I hated losing her friendship, but more than that—because of the attitude she was taking—I wanted to tell her to stuff it.

But finally, since I didn't want to make a bad situation worse, all I did was smile and say, "Have a nice day." And then I turned and walked away and went about my business.

Which—more than likely—was thinking about Gary and about the next time we'd get together.

Which is exactly what I'm doing now. It's Sunday morning, the thirteenth day of my captivity which also happens to be the last day of my captivity because last night—let's hear it for the Brownie Queen!—my strategy finally paid off.

Last night, before I went to bed, my mother came into my room and told me that she'd decided to reduce my sentence by one day. I'd suffered enough, she said, and she hoped I'd learned my lesson.

"Starting Monday morning," she said, "your groundhog days are over."

I thanked her, and then, without thinking, because I was feeling so happy, I promised her I'd mend my ways. I told her that she'd never have to worry about where I was or who I was with and what I was doing, ever again, because from then on, wherever I was and whoever I was with and whatever I was doing, I'd always let her know exactly what I was up to.

But I lied.

Not that I meant to lie. In the heat of the moment, I just forgot that I'd already told my mother I wouldn't be going to church this Sunday because I was going out to the lake with a bunch of kids. I told her that we were going swimming and that I'd be back in plenty of time to get to work by one.

That's what I told her. And as I stand at the kitchen counter on this sunny Sunday morning, swilling my OJ, popping my vitamins, and eyeing the clock on the wall above the sink, that's what she still believes.

It's nine-fifteen and I've told my mother—who's sitting at the kitchen table, sipping coffee over the morning paper—that everybody's getting together at Marlene's at a quarter to ten.

"Don't you think you're pushing the season a little?" she says, looking up from the paper. "The lake is going to be like ice."

She's got a point there.

"If it's too cold," I tell her, "we'll just hang out on the beach and work on our tans."

"How is Marlene?" she asks me.

"Great," I tell her.

"She doesn't pick you up anymore . . ."

"No," I tell her. "She's got a boyfriend."

"Oh," she says. "But she hasn't been over . . ."

"*Nobody's* been over," I remind her. "Remember? I've been grounded."

"Oh, yes," she says. "Well, maybe now you'll have her over some night . . ."

"Yeah," I say, "maybe."

And then, as if I'd just noticed the time, I say, "Whoops! Gotta go!"

"Are you taking the bus to Marlene's?" she asks me.

"Yeah," I tell her.

"Do you have money?" she asks.

"Yes," I tell her.

"Well," she says, "watch out for icebergs."

"Right," I say.

"See you tonight," I say and, grabbing my beach bag, fly out the door.

As I race down the street to the corner—where Gary's sitting in his car, waiting to drive us out to The Campions—I'm feeling kind of bad about lying to my mother, even if it turns out to be only this once.

But I'm also feeling pretty terrific because, right from the beginning, every time I've been with Gary was better than the time before, and I've got a feeling that this time is going to be the best time of all.

Thirty-one

We make love right away—the moment that we arrive at The Campions—without even getting out of the car.

And then we change into our bathing suits and—even though my mother was right and the lake is still just this side of frozen—we go for a swim.

Then, after we finish swimming and horsing around in the water, we wade back to the beach and spread out our beach towels and lie back on them and close our eyes and start soaking up the sun.

At least, that's what *I* do. But while I'm lying there with my eyes closed, I guess Gary gets up and trots over to his car, because the next thing I know, I hear him saying, "Ready for lunch?"

When I open my eyes, there he is, standing over me, holding his ice chest, which I guess he must have gotten out of his trunk.

"I thought we might get hungry," he says, and he sets the ice chest down and opens it up.

Inside the ice chest, in addition to paper plates and plastic knives and forks, I see a bottle of champagne, fried chicken, red potato salad, and a tossed green salad.

"You made this?" I ask him.

He smiles and nods.

"A labor of love," he says.

"Incredible!" I tell him.

He grins.

"You ain't seen nothin' yet," he says.

I wonder what he means, but before I can ask him, he says, "Come on, give me a hand."

So I help him unpack everything and then, when we've got everything set out on our towels, Gary picks up the bottle of champagne and pops the cork. Pouring the bubbling wine into two paper cups, he hands me one and then, lifting his cup in the air, he proposes a toast.

"To the woman who loves me," he says, "and the woman I love—more and more and more."

Which makes me cry.

"I'm sorry," I say.

"Drink up!" he says.

So I do. And as I'm sipping my champagne and snuffling my tears and feeling happier than I've ever felt in my life, Gary says, "Time for the presents!"

And before I can say, *The what?* he jumps to his feet and trots back over to his car and opens the trunk and lifts out this big, gift-wrapped box.

I guess, as he carries the box over to me, he sees the astonished look on my face, because he laughs and shouts, "What could it *be?*"

And I laugh too, because I can't imagine.

And then, a second later, as Gary kneels down on the beach towel opposite me and places the big box on the sand between us, I say, "What's it for?"

Gary smiles and looks into my eyes.

"Just because," he says.

"I love it," I tell him, "whatever it is."

"Open it," he says.

I do, and when the box is opened and I see

what's inside, I can't believe it. "A video camera?!"

Gary smiles and, as if I'd just identified a mysterious object from space, he says, "Very good!"

"Gary! It's wonderful! But how can you—"

"Afford it?" he says.

"Yes," I say. "How *can* you, when—?"

"It's an investment!" he tells me.

"No, really!"

"I got a real good deal on it," he says.

"But Gary—"

"I want you to have it," he says. "Please."

He lifts the camera out of the box and hands it to me.

"Take a look," he says.

I take the camera and lift it to my eye and look through the viewfinder. And what I see—the *way* I see—as I look through the viewfinder makes me gasp.

As I swing the camera around the beach and out over the water, I don't see things the way that they *are,* the way that I see them ordinarily. I see things the way that I *imagine* them, the way I see them in dreams and movies and videos.

Like a director sees, I tell myself.

"I figure," says Gary, "when the video hits and the record takes off, the camera will pay for itself."

I laugh and turn the camera on him and zoom in on his dazzling smile and the sunlight dancing in his eyes.

"Want to read the instructions?" he asks me.

I tell him, Yes, and—even though I hate to part with it for even a second—I lower the camera from my eye.

We read through the instructions together over lunch. But I hardly even taste lunch because I'm so excited about the camera, and I never really finish it because, as soon as we've finished reading the instructions, at Gary's urging, I commence production on my first video.

It isn't much—just Gary out in the water, being attacked by a **huge** but invisible shark, and me, humming the theme from *Jaws* into the camera's built-in microphone—but we have a lot of fun making it, and even Woody Allen had to start somewhere, right?

Thirty-two

Once I'm no longer grounded, my life really takes off. The days and nights that follow that Sunday morning at The Campions are the happiest days and nights of my life. I think of them as my "video days."

I think of them that way because, with our first video behind us, Gary and I set to work putting together our video of "Call Me Susan."

But I also think of them that way because, while we're working on the video, my whole life is like a video—cut to a rocking beat and flowing like a dream from one love scene to the next.

Which doesn't mean that Gary and I spend all of our time together making love, although we do that quite a lot.

But the thing about our love scenes is, they happen whenever we're together, wherever we happen to be, and whatever we happen to be doing.

They happen when we're working with Alan Sinclair, while we're discussing the music for the video, which we plan to record in the mini-recording studio that Alan's built in his attic.

We spend a lot of time up in Alan's attic—working out what the song should sound like and talking about the arrangement and which musicians we should get for the band that's going to back up

Gary's singing—and the whole time we're there, Gary and I are playing love scenes.

And all the time that Gary and I spend at Gary's house, working on the script for the video—working in Gary's kitchen because we can't trust ourselves to keep our minds on business in the living room with the mattress on the floor—we're playing love scenes too.

And when we study together and walk to school together and eat lunch together and walk home from school together and talk together on the phone, whatever it is we're doing, whenever we're together, Gary and I are playing love scenes.

We're like characters in a video. We're inseparable. Nothing can come between us. No one.

Although in real life, a few people try.

Thirty-three

Pamela Rush is a senior, one of the prettiest girls in school, and probably the hottest. She's tall, six feet tall—as tall as Gary—and perfectly proportioned. She has a mass of curly brown hair and mischievous blue eyes and a sly smile which—together with her Olympian body—make her look as fresh as a preacher's daughter and as inviting as a dance hall girl.

In other words, Pamela Rush is nothing less than your typical, young and beautiful, nice-but-naughty dreamgirl, which is why Gary and I agree that she would be the perfect person to play Susan in our video.

But agreeing that we want Pamela to be in our video and persuading her that she wants to be in it are two different things and, since I'm going to be directing the video, it becomes my job to convince Pamela to accept the part.

It isn't easy.

I hardly know Pamela, and she hardly knows me. But nonetheless, one sunny Tuesday afternoon early in May after the last class bell of the day has rung, I catch up with Pamela at her locker.

I say hello and then as I walk with her down the corridor and out into the parking lot, I let her in on my plans for her future.

When I tell her that I'm making a video and I want her to star in it, she's flattered but she's also kind of wary.

She wants to know what kind of video it's going to be, what it's about, and what exactly I want her to do in it.

So, as soon as we reach the parking lot, I invite her to take a seat on the nearest fender, and when she has I take a deep breath and begin telling her the story that Gary and I have worked out—the video that we've conceived as the visual accompaniment to Gary's song.

It goes like this:

Call Me Susan

It's night. The streets are empty. A Greyhound bus pulls into town.

One passenger, The Singer (Gary Everson), gets off the bus. He carries a guitar case in his hand.

As the bus pulls out, The Singer turns and walks down the dark street past a parade of darkened storefronts to an all-night diner.

Inside the diner, The Singer sits down at a booth. He fishes his wallet out of his back pocket and opens it up.

Looking inside his wallet, we see that The Singer has only one dollar.

As a pretty waitress, The Waitress (Pamela Rush), arrives at the booth, she sees this too.

Looking up from his wallet, The Singer discovers The Waitress, waiting to take his order. He smiles and orders coffee.

The Waitress smiles and goes off to place the order.

The Singer watches The Waitress, as she goes off.

We fade to BLACK.

We fade in on The Waitress, returning to the booth and serving The Singer his coffee.

The Singer smiles and says, "Thank you."

The Waitress smiles and says, "You're welcome."

The Waitress turns and walks away.

The Singer sips his coffee and watches The Waitress, as she goes off.

We fade to BLACK.

We fade in on the booth. It is empty. The Singer is gone. But next to his empty coffee cup, he's left his last dollar bill.

We discover The Waitress, as she discovers the dollar bill. She is surprised and touched.

As a Second Customer calls for service, The Waitress quickly picks up The Singer's empty cup, pockets the dollar bill, calls "Hold your horses!" and goes off to wait on the Second Customer.

We fade to BLACK.

We fade in on the all-night diner as The Waitress walks out the door and discovers The Singer waiting for her.

The Waitress isn't surprised. And she isn't delighted. But she's curious.

We fade to BLACK.

We fade in on the waitress's living room.

178

A fire crackles and burns in the fireplace. The Waitress and The Singer sit on the floor before it. The Waitress sips wine and looks on as The Singer plays his guitar and sings his song for her.

We fade to BLACK.

We fade in on the waitress's bedroom, the waitress's bed. The Waitress and The Singer are in bed, making love—slowly and beautifully.

We fade to BLACK.

We fade in on the waitress's kitchen, early the next morning. The Singer sits alone at the kitchen table, sipping coffee and thinking serious thoughts. He looks up as The Waitress enters.

The Waitress is barefoot and dressed in a loose-fitting, plain, but very flattering robe.

The Singer smiles when he sees her, but The Waitress doesn't return his smile. The smile fades from The Singer's face as The Waitress walks to the stove and pours herself a cup of coffee.

The Singer watches The Waitress as she carries her coffee to the table and sits in the chair, opposite him.

The Waitress looks across the table at The Singer and studies his eyes.

The Singer looks across the table at The Waitress and studies her eyes.

After a long moment, The Waitress smiles.

As she does, The Singer smiles back at her.

Then, at the exact same moment, The

Waitress and The Singer reach across the table and take each other's hands and, with their free hands, still smiling and looking into each other's eyes, they lift their cups and sip their coffee.

The End.

Pamela doesn't like it.

Well, she *likes* it. But she tells me—even though she thinks that starring in a video might be fun—she isn't about to take off her clothes and climb into bed with some guy and make love to him, while I stand there with my camera and tape her.

But when I assure her that my intentions are strictly honorable, and that she won't have to get completely undressed for the love scene (because I can use sheets and shadows to hide the bikini that she'll be wearing) and that she won't have to do much more than neck a little and roll around in bed, she smiles and says, "Who with?"

So I tell her, "With The Singer."

"Who is who?" she asks.

"The guy who wrote the song," I tell her.

"Who is who?" she asks again.

"Gary Everson."

She smiles and says, "What's the song like?"

I don't like the way she smiles. But it *is* the way that Susan would smile if she were interested in a boy.

So I smile back at her, and I say, "You have to hear it."

"Okay," she says. "But I'm not promising I'll do it."

"Wait till you hear the song," I tell her.

Which she does.

That same night.

In the finished basement at her house.

And when Gary finishes playing and singing "Call Me Susan" for her, Pamela laughs and says, "That's me, all right."

Gary smiles and says, "Do you like it?"

"It's great," she says. "And I *love* the way you sing it."

"Really?" he asks her.

"Like you've *been* there," she says.

"He *has!*" I tell her.

But Pamela isn't paying any attention to me. She's too busy looking at Gary and letting him know how much she likes what she sees.

"What do I wear?" she asks him. "Aside from a bikini?"

"You'll do it?" Gary asks her.

"Why not?" she says.

And that's that.

At least that's what I tell myself. Only, as far as Pamela's concerned, that's just the beginning. Starting the next day with our first rehearsal, she picks up right where she left off the night before, flirting with Gary every chance she gets.

Gary treats it as a joke and that's what I try to do too.

But I don't like it. I mean, I'd be a fool if I wasn't worried about Gary's falling for somebody as great-looking as Pamela, especially when somebody as great-looking as Pamela is practically throwing herself at him.

But I tell myself, *That's just the way that girls like Pamela and Susan are, and if that's the kind of girl I want in my video, then this is the kind of thing I'm going to have to put up with.*

So I keep my peace and hold my tongue and go along with the joke.

But as the days go by and we finish rehearsing and start taping our first scenes, Pamela gets more and more obvious, and I find it harder and harder to just laugh it off.

And finally, after we've been taping scenes for about a week, it gets to the point where I'm about to tell Pamela to either cut it out or take a walk.

But suddenly it hits me that would be the worst thing that I could do, because so far, through some kind of miracle, the more that Pamela's thrown herself at Gary, the less interested in her he's become.

I mean, even if Gary was tempted at first, by now Pamela's flirting has become as big a drag to him as it is to me.

So, I tell myself, *the more that Pamela flirts with Gary, the less I have to worry about her coming between Gary and me.*

And I keep my mouth shut.

And if I smile the next time that Pamela calls Gary "Handsome" and "accidentally" brushes against him, it's because I'm thinking, *Nice try, Pamela,* and I'm telling myself, *As long as I go along with the joke, the joke is on her.*

Thirty-four

Janice is about the last person I'd expect to try to come between Gary and me. But one day, while Gary's off running some errand or other, I see her sitting by herself in the cafeteria and, even though we haven't talked much since our shoot-out in the cafeteria, I decide to sit with her.

Janice doesn't know that Gary and I have been making a video. In fact, even though Gary and Alan have already recorded their song and I've been taping the scenes that go with it for over a week now, except for the people who are actually working on it, all of whom Gary has sworn to secrecy, nobody at school has the slightest idea of what we've been up to.

But the video is the furthest thing from my mind as I slide my lunch tray onto Janice's table and pull up a chair across from her.

What's on my mind is the look on Janice's face. She looks so sad and heartbroken that I have to ask her what's wrong.

Lifting her sad eyes to mine, Janice looks across the table at me and, in a voice that's practically dripping with sympathy, says, "I heard about Gary and Pamela."

I almost burst out laughing, because I've been with Pamela and Gary whenever they've been together, and I know, as hard as she's tried—and precisely *because* she's tried as hard as she's tried—Pamela's gotten nowhere with Gary.

But since I can't wait to hear what Janice has to say, I force myself to keep a straight face and, acting surprised and really concerned, I look across the table at her and say, "What did you hear?"

Janice looks alarmed.

"Haven't you heard?" she asks me.

I shake my head.

I can see by the way that Janice squirms that she wasn't planning on being the one who broke the news to me, but after a moment, because she apparently feels that it's her "duty" as my "friend" to tell me what she thought I already knew, she shrugs and says, "Just that they're going out."

"Oh," I say, smiling like I couldn't care less, "is *that* all?"

Janice doesn't know what to make of that.

"You *knew?*" she asks me.

"Sure," I say. "Gary tells me everything."

"And you don't *care?*" she asks.

I shrug.

"They're probably doing it," I tell her. "But I don't think it's serious."

"Angelica!"

Janice's jaw drops open and her eyes go wide.

I take a second to bask in the glow of Janice's admiration, and then, as I dig into my meat loaf, I say, "So what's up with you?"

Which—if she was trying to come between Gary and me by spreading rumors about Gary and Pamela—is about as far as Janice gets.

184

Thirty-five

Maybe I underestimated Pamela, or maybe I overestimated Gary, or maybe I just got it all wrong.

All I know is when we get around to taping the love scene—at my house, in my mother's bedroom, because I want to use my mother's beautiful old four-poster bed—things don't work out the way I planned.

Because we're using my house and my mother's bedroom and my mother's bed, I've got to get the love scene set up and taped and cleaned up after between the time that I get out of school at two-thirty and the time that my mother usually gets home around six o'clock.

So that's what I'm trying to do.

It's a little before three o'clock on a rainy Thursday afternoon. Gary's lying on my mother's bed, wearing a skin-tight bathing suit. Pamela is in my mother's bathroom, changing into her bikini. And I'm fussing with the lights—which we've rented—and wondering how much longer Pamela's going to be.

I'm anxious to get started, although—I have to admit—I'm not exactly looking forward to seeing Pamela in a bikini.

On the other hand, if I *have to* see Pamela in a

bikini, I'd prefer to see her in *all of it,* instead of just the *bottom half* which, when she finally steps out of my mother's bathroom, is *all that she's wearing!*

I can't believe it! I can't believe *them!* I mean, I knew Pamela was built, but—God!—her breasts are like young honeydews and her nipples are like ripe raspberries!

I feel like shouting, *Put those things away!* But all I say is, "That isn't necessary."

But Pamela isn't listening to me. She's looking at Gary, who—believe me!—is looking at her.

"For inspiration," she says.

Gary smiles.

"Are you inspired?" I ask him.

He doesn't answer right away. He just keeps looking at what he's looking at.

But then, after a second, still looking and still smiling, he shakes his head and says, "Ain't nothin' like the real thing."

Pamela laughs.

I glower.

"Fine," I say. "Let's go."

I'm *pissed!*

Thoroughly.

But then, when Pamela hops into bed with Gary, and I start taping them, and I see how truly "inspired" Gary actually is, I get furious! Because it seems to me the way that Gary's throwing himself into kissing Pamela, body and soul, *he isn't acting at all!* In fact, after I've taped all of the kissing and rolling around that I need, I can't get him to stop! I have to scream, "Cut!" three times, before he even slows down!

But by then, it doesn't matter. I've already decided that I'm through with Gary. I'm going to finish the video for him, because I said I would, but after that, I'm history!

So, when the action finally *does* grind to a halt, I can't wait for Pamela to get dressed and get out.

And then, when she's gone, I can't wait for Gary to do the same.

"Come on," I tell him. "I've got to straighten up."

He's still lying on my mother's bed.

"How'd it look?" he asks me.

"Fine," I tell him.

"That's all?"

"Great," I tell him.

"What's wrong?" he asks me.

"Nothing's wrong."

"Was I too convincing?"

"Yes!"

Gary smiles and holds his hand out to me.

"Come here," he says.

"No!"

"You wanted it to look real, didn't you?"

"I didn't want it to *be* real!"

He laughs.

"She's not my type," he says.

"Ha!"

"Are you jealous?"

"Jealous?"

Gary smiles.

"Good," he says. "Because you haven't got anything to be jealous about."

"I don't?"

He shakes his head.

"I saved all my best stuff for you," he says.

"You shouldn't have bothered," I tell him.

"Come here," he says. "I'll show you."

He reaches out and tries to take my hand, but I pull it away.

"My mother's coming home!"

"When?"

"Soon!"

"Come here."

He reaches out and grabs my hand and tries to pull me down to the bed with him, but I hold back. "You said you loved me," I remind him.

"I do," he says. "I love you."

"Only?" I ask him.

"Only," he says, "and always."

Is he lying to me? Or is he telling me the truth? I search his eyes, as if I could see into his heart.

"Convince me," I tell him.

He smiles and pulls me down onto the bed with him and kisses me.

And before long, he's convinced me.

Thoroughly.

Which—as hard as she was trying to come between Gary and me—is about as far as Pamela gets.

My mother is next.

Thirty-six

I couldn't be any higher.

It's Saturday night and we've invited everybody up to Alan's attic to see the finished video and I'm positively soaring.

Just a couple of days ago, I was anything but. After the stunt that Pamela pulled when we taped the love scene, I wasn't exactly looking forward to taping the final scene with her.

But the truth is, when we actually got around to taping it, it worked out perfectly— at least, from my point of view—because Gary stunk

At least, at first.

I mean, as The Singer on the morning after he'd spent the night before making slow and beautiful love to Susan, Gary was supposed to act like he was totally in love with Pamela.

But the morning that we taped the scene— downstairs, in Alan's kitchen—even though Pamela actually looked even better in her loosely-tied robe than she had in the lesser half of her bikini, Gary looked like he couldn't have cared less.

I kept taping the scene over and over, trying to get Gary to put some feeling into the way he looked at Pamela. But the more I taped, the less Gary seemed to care, until finally, there was no point in going on.

So I stopped taping and, taking Gary aside, I told him straight out, if he couldn't get an I-adore-you look in his eyes when he looked at Pamela, then everything we'd taped up to that point—as good as it might be—wouldn't amount to anything. It would just turn out to be a big buildup to an even bigger letdown.

Turning his back to Pamela and speaking in a whisper so she couldn't hear, Gary said, "How am I supposed to act like I'm in love with *her*, when I'm nuts about *you?*"

Which had to be my number one, favorite question of all time.

But I didn't throw my arms around Gary and kiss him, like I would have if he were just my lover and I weren't his director. I just shrugged like there was nothing to it and glanced over at Pamela and said, "Just pretend she's me."

Which made Gary burst out laughing. And then, he threw his arms around me and kissed me, which was great. And then, glancing over at Pamela, he shook his head like, *This isn't going to be easy,* and he said, "I'll do the best I can."

And *I* laughed. And when I finished, I looked over at Pamela and said, "Okay. Let's try it again."

Which we did. And when we did—and Gary looked at Pamela with a little of the love that he felt for me—it looked just right.

And tonight, here at Alan's, as the scene and the song and the whole video all come to an end, everybody in Alan's attic—Alan, Mark, Ratso, Richie, and Robbie (the band that backed up Gary on the music track), the girls who they brought with them (whose names I didn't catch), Pamela (who showed up with Brian Avery, of all people!),

Donnie Alexander (who played the Second Customer in the all-night diner scene), Aurora (Donnie Alexander's girlfriend), weird Wayne Shuster (who came alone)—everybody in the place (including Gary and me) bursts out cheering and applauding.

And suddenly, I don't know what it is, but that sound, the sound of everybody clapping and cheering, it feels like it's exactly the thing I've been looking for all my life.

I mean, except for Gary, saying, "I love you," hearing that sound makes me happy like nothing else ever has before.

It makes me feel like a baby bird must feel at the moment her mother pushes her out of her nest and she realizes, *My God! I can fly!*

And now, with everybody telling me and Gary (and Alan and Pamela and Donnie and the band) how great the video is, and how great the song is, and asking us to play it again, I'm hovering somewhere high above Alan's attic. And Alan hasn't even begun passing his dope around yet.

Which, before long—Alan being Alan—he does. And after I've taken a couple tokes of Alan's "primo," I'm so high, I'm teetering on the brink of weightlessness.

But I get even higher, because not long after that, Gary and I leave Alan's and go back to Gary's house. And before we make love and after we make love and even while we make love, Gary keeps weaving this beautiful fantasy for me, telling me how he's going to get our video to an agent, who will get it on MTV. And how this agent will sell the record to a big record company. And how the video will hit the airwaves and the record will zoom up to the top of the charts. And how we'll both become stars and go out touring all over the country and all around the world. And how, after a while, we'll get married and live on a big estate and have children and *they'll* write songs and make videos and go out touring all over the country and all around the world.

And the thing is, while he's going on like that, Gary half believes it. And, as high as I am, I half believe it too. *If not this time with this video,* I tell myself, *then maybe next time with the next one?*

How can Fate deny the dreams of two talented kids in love? I ask myself.

I tell myself, *No way!* And I laugh out loud.

That's how high I am. In fact, by the time I leave Gary's, even though it's half-past twelve and I'm already half an hour late getting home, I'm so deep into space and so far out among the stars that I couldn't care less.

But when we pull up in front of my house and I see that my mother's home and waiting up for me, I come down to earth so fast, I almost get the bends.

Except the thing is, when I get inside the house and find my mother in the kitchen, listening to the radio and sipping a glass of wine, all she does is smile at me and say, "Hi," like she's glad to see me, even though I'm over half an hour late.

And when I apologize for being late—and explain that I've been showing a video that I made to a bunch of my friends and I lost track of the time— all my mother does is nod and smile, like she understands and it's okay.

I can't believe it. In fact, I'm so surprised that my mother isn't angry at me for getting home late that it never occurs to me that I should be angry at *her* for not asking me to tell her about my video—

which she doesn't—even though this is the first time that I've ever mentioned it to her.

I mean, you'd think she'd be interested. But she doesn't say a word. She just lets it go by, as if it weren't anything, as if *I* weren't.

But—like I said—I'm so relieved that she isn't angry, I barely notice. And now, as if she hasn't already surprised me enough, my mother says, "Can I get you something?"

"That's okay," I tell her.

But she's already getting up from the table.

"A Coke?" she says. "Or some milk? Or a glass of wine?"

Jesus! I think. *What's going on?* I mean, my mother always drinks wine, but she's never offered any to me before. So of course I say, "Sure!"

Smiling, my mother walks over to the cupboard, gets me a wine glass, carries it over to the table, pours me a glass of wine, hands it to me and says, "There's no sense pretending you're a baby anymore."

Which *really* blows my mind! I mean, my mother's been pretending I was a baby since I *was* a baby. It's hard to believe that suddenly, from out of nowhere, she's decided to stop. And if she *hasn't*, then why is she pretending that she *has?* Why has she offered me a glass of wine?

"Want to sit for a while?" she asks me.

I'm as suspicious as I am curious, but nonetheless, I say, "Sure," and I pull out a chair and sit down at the kitchen table.

My mother takes a chair across from me and the next thing I know—just as if we were a couple of old girlfriends settling down to a nice chat—she raises her glass to me, and I raise my glass to her, and we smile at one another and sip our wine.

"Mmm . . ." I say.

"French," says my mother.

"It's good," I say.

"*Too* good," she says. "You have to watch yourself or before you know it—" She crosses her eyes and sticks out her tongue.

Which makes me laugh and reconsider.

Maybe I've got it all wrong, I tell myself. *Maybe she isn't up to anything. Maybe she's just decided to loosen up a little.*

But then she starts.

"How's Gary?" she says.

"Fine," I tell her.

"You're seeing an awful lot of him, aren't you?"

"Yes," I say.

"But you're not going steady with him or anything?"

"No."

"So, you *can* go out with other boys?"

"If I want to."

"Well, don't you think you *should?*"

"No."

"But aren't you a little young to be limiting yourself to just one boy?"

"Old girlfriends" my foot! She isn't playing "old girlfriends," I tell myself. *She's playing "prosecuting attorney"!*

But somehow I manage to hold my temper. Looking my mother square in the eye, I say, "If I remember correctly, *you* were about my age when *you* started limiting yourself to just one boy."

"Yes," she says. "And look how *that* worked out."

She looks so sad, so defeated, it *kills* me! I want to cry. I want to scream.

"Anyway," she says, "we were in love."

"So are *we!*" I tell her.

She looks at me like I'm crazy.

"You've only *known* Gary—"

"Six weeks, tomorrow night," I tell her.

She laughs.

"That's no time at all," she says.

"It's time enough," I tell her.

"I want you to start seeing other boys."

"Why?!"

"Because you've got your whole future ahead of you, and there's a world full of boys!"

"None of them are Gary."

"Did he tell you about his father?"

"What?!"

"Did he?"

"Tell me what?"

"That he's disappeared?" she says. "That he's a deadbeat, who just got out of town a step ahead of the police?"

"That isn't what *happened!*"

"Don't tell *me* what happened!" she says. "I happen to work in a law office! And I happen to know what's going on in this town. I know about all the people who want to get their hands on Ray Everson. The people whose goods he took. And services. And money. Ray Everson is a shady operator."

"He is *not!*"

"Oh?" says my mother. "Then where is he?"

"In San Diego!"

Shit! I think. *I promised Gary I wouldn't say anything to anybody. He'll kill me!*

"I'm not supposed to tell you that," I add as quickly as I can. "He's raising money. But you can't tell anybody. Promise."

My mother just looks at me for a second. And

then she nods—just once—and says, "You'll start seeing other boys?"

I can't believe it!

"That's blackmail!" I tell her.

She nods again—just once—and says, "I think, for your own good, you should start seeing less of Gary."

"And if I don't?" I ask her.

She shrugs.

"You *wouldn't!*"

She shrugs again.

Jesus! I think. *She could! She actually could!*

"I'll think about it," I tell her, although I don't intend to. "Okay?"

"Think hard," she says.

"You won't say anything?"

She smiles.

"I'm not a policeman," she says.

I say, "Thank you," and I heave a sigh of relief. But my mother isn't done.

"Have you slept with him?"

"Mother!"

"Sex isn't everything."

"I didn't think it *was!*" I tell her. "I thought *love* was everything!"

She nods and says, "I did too."

I don't know what to say to that, because I feel so incredibly sorry for my mother, sorry because she's lost her faith in love and sorry because she doesn't realize that my love for Gary is so deep and so strong and so good that no matter what she does, she'll never be able to keep us apart.

Thirty-seven

I'm sitting in the bleachers out by the baseball field. It's Monday afternoon, and I'm having lunch with Marlene.

It was her idea. Before she called me yesterday morning, I'd thought that our last conversation might actually turn out to be our last conversation.

But when she asked me if I'd meet her out here today, I thought she might be in trouble and need someone to talk to, so I agreed to meet her.

But so far, since I got here, all we've talked about is stuff in general—school, and the weather, and who's supposedly going out with whom—and I'm down to dessert, a peach that I brought from home, and lunch hour's almost over.

But, I tell myself, *If that's all she wants to talk about, it's okay with me.*

As I bite into my peach, Marlene says, "Does Alan Sinclair always smoke pot?"

"Huh?" I say.

"You've been hanging around with him, somebody said—you and Gary. I just wondered."

"Oh," I say. "Yeah, I have. We have. A little. What did you want to know?"

"If Alan smokes pot all the time, like everybody says he does."

"Oh, right," I say. I'm not sure it's any of

Marlene's business what Alan Sinclair does, but I shrug and say, "I don't know about all the time, but quite a bit, I guess. Why?"

Marlene takes a deep breath and lets it out and shakes her head and says nothing.

So I say, "Do you think there's something wrong with that?"

Marlene shakes her head again and says nothing again.

I'm beginning to wonder why she brought it up. But then, after a second, she says, "Do you know all the pot that everybody's been smoking since last summer?"

"Yeah?" I say.

"Where do you think they get it?" she asks me.

"Huh?"

"Who do you think sells it to them?"

I shrug and say, "I don't know."

"I do," she says.

"So," I say. "Who?"

"Gary."

I look at her like she's lost her mind.

"Gary?!"

"I just found out yesterday."

"Really?"

"I didn't want to tell you—"

I blow up.

"The hell you didn't!"

"I didn't!"

"It doesn't matter," I tell her, "because it isn't true!"

"It is!"

"Who says it is?"

"Ronnie Crosby, for one."

Him again!

"How would he know?"

"He's bought it from Gary."

"He's a liar!"

"He's not the only one."

"Really!"

"*Everybody* gets it from Gary."

"Who's *everybody?*"

"Dwyer," she says.

I laugh.

"Dwyer?"

Marlene nods.

"Where do you think he got the stuff that he brought to Gayle's that time?"

"From Gary, I suppose."

"Uh-huh."

"Bullshit!"

"Ask him."

"Dwyer?!"

"Gary."

"I will!"

"I'm sorry."

"I'll bet!"

"I thought you'd want to know."

"Is that what you wanted to talk to me about?"

"Yes."

"Well," I tell her, "you have. And now that you have, you can go fuck yourself!"

I shout it, and I get up on my feet, and I storm out of there because I really hate Marlene, and I don't want her to see me crying. And because *somehow I know*—Jesus! It's so awful to admit, but God damn it!—*somehow I know that what she's told me is the truth!*

Thirty-eight

I'm waiting for Gary. I'm sitting on his front steps, waiting for him to come home from school. I never went back. After lunch, after Marlene, I never went back to school.

I couldn't. I couldn't stop crying and I couldn't tell anybody *why* I was crying, so I just took off for the hills behind the high school.

It's all country out there, like it is all around Waterford. There are hills and open fields, deep woods and running streams all around the edge of town. I suppose a stranger could get lost out there.

But when I was a kid, my friends and I used to ramble all around the edge of town, playing kid games—fantasies that we'd make up and act out, where we'd pretend that we were visitors from another planet exploring a new world, or survivors of a terrible disaster lost in the wilderness and searching for a way out. Things like that.

But anyway, the point is I know the country around Waterford pretty well. It's like an old friend, a friend who—I figured out—could hide me from the world while I made my way from the hills behind the high school to the open fields around Gary's house.

So that's how I got here, to Gary's house—the

back way, through the woods and fields. I didn't see a soul and nobody saw me.

Thank goodness. I was a mess when I started out. If I'd run into a bear, he'd have taken one look at me and turned and run away.

I was fierce and I was furious—at Marlene for telling me about Gary, at myself for believing what she'd told me, and at Gary of course, most of all, for doing what Marlene said and what I believed he'd been doing.

But somehow, as I walked—cutting through the woods, picking my way over half-remembered trails, weaving my way through mazes of trees, noticing some birds, a chipmunk—somehow, like an old friend, the country soothed and steadied me.

So, by the time that I got here, I'd pretty much sorted out my feelings, and I was pretty together, considering—until I spotted the police car coming up the street.

I panicked. *They're looking for Gary!* I thought, as if the police had found out about Gary at the same time that I did. *They've come to arrest him!*

Which was ridiculous, I know. But what can I tell you? I was *nuts!*

The police car pulled to a stop at the end of Gary's driveway. I froze and waited for a policeman to climb out of the car or to roll down his window and call me over.

But nobody budged.

After a while I got curious. So I bent down to see if I could get a look inside the police car—which I could—and there, sitting behind the wheel and looking back at me, I saw Officer Glenn Van Dyke.

The weird thing was, when I saw him, I actually

felt relieved, because I figured, if it was Van Dyke, he was probably just looking for Gary's father. *The senior criminal in the Everson family,* I told myself. Which, even under the circumstances, I found oddly amusing.

But I wasn't amused for long because I quickly reminded myself that I wasn't being fair to Gary's father. Or to Gary, for that matter.

I mean, I had no *reason* to believe what Marlene told me. I had no *reason* to believe that Gary was dealing drugs. It was just a *feeling* that I had—that I *have*—and I feel *lousy* about it!

But anyway, Van Dyke . . . He didn't do anything. He just sat there at the end of the driveway until I guess he got bored, and then, he just shifted into gear and drove off.

Good riddance! I thought as I watched him go. But for some reason, once he'd gone, I felt terribly alone.

That was about twenty minutes ago. Van Dyke was my last visitor.

Since then, I've been sitting here, wondering what I'm going to say when—and if—Gary finally shows up. I have to ask him if it's true. I have to tell Gary what Marlene told me and—without letting him suspect that I believe it—I have to ask him if it's true.

I have to give Gary a chance to laugh in my face. And tease me. I can just hear him saying, "We've been reading *The Waterford Enquirer* again, haven't we, girl?"

Except, what if he admits it? God! What if he's actually been selling drugs?

I mean, it's one thing to smoke dope occasionally, if that's what you want to do, but getting other people to smoke it, taking the chance that you might be starting them down the road to harder drugs, to serious addictions, to wasted lives—that's *another thing*, entirely. A terrible thing, the way I see it.

But what will I do, if that's what Gary's been doing? What will I do then? Tell him that he has to quit? Tell him that he has to stop dealing drugs or stop seeing me? That he can't do both?

But what if he tells me that he won't stop dealing drugs? What then? Do I just say good-bye? Even though I love Gary with all my heart? Do I just say good-bye and never see him again for as long as I live?

I'd rather die. I *mean* it.

Another car. It's heading this way.

I don't recognize the car, but after a second, it pulls up in front of the house, and Gary gets out.

When he sees me sitting on his front steps, he greets me with a smile that's as sweet as a kiss.

As the car pulls out, he calls to me, "I wondered where you were."

As he heads up the driveway, I call back to him, "I was here."

As he crosses from the driveway to the front landing, he says, "Doing what?"

"Waiting for you," I tell him.

He sits down on the steps beside me.

"Yeah," he says. "I see. But why?"

"I want to buy some dope."

Gary looks at me, like I must be crazy, And because I never planned to just throw it at him like that, I'm thinking, *I must be crazy!*

But then, Gary laughs and says, "I'm afraid you've come to the wrong place."

"Have I?" I ask him.

He nods and says, "You might try Dominick's."

"Have I?" I ask him again.

Gary looks at me, looks into my eyes. He can see I'm not joking. I hold my breath, waiting to hear what he'll say, praying that he'll say the right thing.

"Who told you?" he says.

The wrong thing.

"Does it matter?" I ask him.

"Yes," he says.

"Marlene."

"Marlene . . . ?"

"Is it true?" I ask him.

He doesn't answer. Instead, he gets to his feet and offers me his hand.

"Come on inside," he says.

I don't take his hand. Instead, I look up at him and say, "It is, isn't it?"

"Come on," he says.

"No!" I tell him.

"Please."

"Answer my question!"

He looks at me. And he nods.

"Gary! Why?"

I can't hold back my tears.

Gary kneels down beside me and puts his arm around my shoulders.

"Calm down," he says.

"Calm down?!" I cry.

"Come on," he says.

He gets to his feet.

"Please," he says.

He offers me his hand.

As I take his hand and get to my feet, I say, "Why?"

"It's a long story," he says.

"Is it a *true* story?" I ask him.

He looks at me, like I've hurt him, like I've slapped his face.

I feel sick to my stomach.

"Yes," he says.

And he turns away from me.

I stand there, loving him and hating him, as he unlocks his front door and swings it open.

Thirty-nine

I'm not sitting on the mattress. I'm sitting on the orange crate. Bawling.

Gary's gone off to look for some Kleenex. I don't want him to see me like this when he gets back.

I struggle to get a hold of myself. But just when I've nearly succeeded, I hear Gary calling from the hallway, "Are you sure you wouldn't rather borrow a handkerchief?"

And as I look up and see him walking back into the room, carrying a roll of toilet paper, I shake my head and start up all over again. Bawling.

Gary hands me the roll of toilet paper and squats down on the floor in front of me. As I set to work, blowing my nose and mopping up my tears, he looks up at me and says, "It isn't that big a deal."

"How can you *say* that?" I wail.

"It's only smoke!" he says, like that's nothing.

"It's against the law!" I remind him.

"So is drinking underage," he tells me.

"It's different!" I say. "And you know it!"

"Yes," he says. "Drinking is dangerous and smoking dope isn't."

I look at him.

"*Is* it?" he asks me.

I shake my head.

"I don't know," I tell him.

Gary smiles, like I should know better and I might as well admit it.

"Come on!" he says.

"That isn't the point!" I tell him. "The point isn't whether dope is worse for you than alcohol is. The point is you can get arrested for selling dope! You can get thrown in jail! In prison!"

Gary smiles and shakes his head.

"I'm very careful," he tells me.

"How careful can you *be?*" I ask him.

"Extremely," he says. "I only sell small amounts, never more than an ounce. And I only sell to people I know, people who I can trust to keep their mouths shut."

"Like who?"

He smiles and shakes his head.

"They trust me to keep *my* mouth shut, too," he says.

"Where do you get it?" I ask him.

But he won't tell me that either. Not that I care, really. I only care that wherever he gets the marijuana from, whoever sells it to him is probably a dangerous person. Probably a professional criminal, someone who carries a gun.

But Gary tells me he isn't afraid of the guy he gets his marijuana from. He calls him his supplier. He tells me he has no reason to be afraid of him.

"As long as my books balance," he says.

"You keep *books?*" I ask him.

He laughs.

"Not exactly," he says. "I keep the dope and the money that I get for it. And as long I've got enough money to cover the dope that I've sold and enough dope to cover the dope that I haven't sold, when my supplier comes around to collect—"

"He comes *here?*"

Gary nods.

"You *keep it* here?"

Gary nods again.

"The safest place in the world," he says.

I look at him like he's crazy.

"Come here," he says. "I'll show you something."

As he gets to his feet, I try to imagine what he could show me that would convince me that this unfurnished house in the middle of an open field is the "safest place in the world."

An armed guard? A pet lion? I can't imagine what it could be. But I'm curious enough to get up off the orange crate and follow Gary out of the living room and down the hallway to the wine cellar.

He stops as he reaches the wine cellar door. He reaches for the doorknob. He looks back over his shoulder at me, like he's having second thoughts about showing me whatever he's about to show me.

And then, as if he's decided it's all right, he opens the door.

I look inside the wine cellar. I don't know what I expect to see, but all I *do* see is what I saw before—racks of wine bottles from the ceiling to the floor.

But now, reaching into the wine cellar, Gary removes a couple bottles of wine from the wine rack and shows me, hidden behind the wine bottles and mounted against the wall, a black box with a row of blinking red lights.

And then, as if he were a salesman on late-night TV, he points at the black box and says, "*That* is the control center for the most advanced electronic security system that money can buy. A foolproof, easy-to-operate security system that protects your cherished valuables and provides your loved ones with the kind of first-rate security that they deserve.''

From the way he looks at me when he finishes, I guess that Gary expects me to laugh.

But when he sees that I'm not amused, he just shrugs and goes back to being himself. As he shoves the bottles back into the wine rack and closes the wine cellar door, he says, ''The point is, nobody gets into the house unless I want them to.''

As we start heading back to the living room, he says, ''And if anybody tries to break in, an alarm goes off down at the police station and five minutes later the culprit is hip deep in uniformed officers of the law.''

''Great!'' I say. ''So they arrest the guy for stealing your marijuana—''

Gary laughs, but I go on.

''And then they turn around and arrest *you* for having it here in the first place.''

''No way!'' he says. ''Because even if a burglar *did* get in here, there's no way he could figure out where I've stashed my stash. Nobody could.''

As we walk into the living room, I say, ''Not even the police?''

As I reclaim my place on the orange crate, Gary says, ''Not even the police.''

As he sits down on the floor in front of me, he says, ''When they built this place, my father had them build in a hidden safe-storage box for his personal papers and things.''

He shakes his head and smiles and says, ''Sherlock Holmes couldn't find it.''

''Sherlock Holmes isn't Glenn Van Dyke,'' I remind him.

Which breaks Gary up.

But I'm not kidding. Holmes is a character in a book, but Van Dyke is for real.

"Nobody could find it," says Gary.

"What about a specially trained dog?" I ask him. He shrugs.

"Maybe Benji," he says.

"Where is it?" I ask him.

I'm not sure that I want to know, but I have to ask.

Gary looks me in the eye.

"Can I trust you?" he asks me.

I look him back in the eye.

"I've trusted you," I remind him.

"Do you think I should have told you about it? About what I was doing?"

"I don't know," I tell him. "Maybe."

"I never thought about it," he says. "I mean, I guess it crossed my mind, but I thought you'd just get upset, and I didn't want to upset you."

"Oh!" I say. "Thanks a lot!"

Gary reaches out and takes my hand and looks into my eyes.

"I shouldn't have let you find out the way you did," he says. "You're right. I was a jerk. I'm sorry."

And the thing is, I believe him. I believe that he's sorry. Maybe I shouldn't, but I do.

"So," I say, "where is it?"

Gary smiles and says, "Right in front of you."

I think, *What's right in front of me?*

I'm sitting with my back to the big bay window, facing . . .

"The fireplace?" I guess.

Gary smiles and nods.

"But even if you knew that," he says, "you still couldn't find it. Take a look."

I accept his challenge. I get up from the orange crate and walk over to the fireplace. It looks like a regular fireplace, only it's a lot bigger than most and a lot prettier. It's made out of fieldstone and trimmed with cedar, just like the outside of the house.

I study it closely, poring over it from the mantel to the floor, searching the fieldstone facing for telltale seams, feeling along the mortared grooves between the fieldstones for a hidden button or switch.

But after a couple of minutes, when I've concluded my examination, I haven't found a trace of a hidden safe-storage box—not a clue.

"Open the flue," Gary suggests.

I look inside the fireplace opening and there, at the top of the opening, right in the center, I see this hammered wrought-iron lever.

"This?" I ask Gary.

"Yeah," he says. "That opens the shutter to the chimney. You push it away from you. Go ahead."

I push the lever away from me and, as I do, I hear a dull, metallic clank.

"Now close it," he says.

I pull the lever back to me and, again, I hear the dull, metallic clank.

"So," says Gary, "*now* do you know where I hide my stash?"

I shake my head.

Gary grins.

"You're so close," he says, "but you're still miles away."

"Are you going to tell me?" I ask him.

He looks at me.

"Are you sure you want to know?"

I'm not sure. Not really. Part of me is curious to

know where the safe-storage box is hidden, and part of me recoils at the idea of seeing what's hidden inside it.

But there's another part of me, a part of me that still can't believe that Gary's been selling marijuana and won't believe that he's got a bunch of it stored in a hidden safe-storage box unless I actually see it with my own eyes.

And it's that part of me that I'm listening to, when I nod and tell Gary, "Yes, I'm sure."

He nods.

"Okay," he says. "Open the flue again."

Reaching into the fireplace again, I grip the wrought-iron lever, push it away from me and hear the flue opening.

"Now," he says, "put your fingers on the bottom edge of the lever and push it straight up."

I do what Gary says and, as I push the lever up, I feel it slide an inch or two deeper into its housing.

"Hold it in," says Gary, "and push it as far to the left as you can."

Holding the lever in, I slide it about six inches to the left.

"Now," says Gary, "very slowly, bring it halfway back toward the center."

Very slowly, I push the lever halfway and— *click*—two of the fieldstones, a joined pair of them, pop out from under the mantel.

As if he were astonished, Gary says, "You've found it!"

I look over at the two fieldstones, sticking out from the fireplace facing.

"Slide it open," Gary tells me. "It's a drawer."

I slip my hand under the fieldstones and slide them toward me. It *is* a drawer, a drawer about six inches deep and two feet across.

"My stash," says Gary.

"Oh, God!" I say.

I can feel tears coming to my eyes and sobs jumping in my chest as I look down into the drawer.

It's packed—filled to the rim—with marijuana. There are, maybe, two dozen plastic baggies filled with the stuff. And a half-filled carton of Bambu cigarette papers. And a scale. And a big envelope, held together with a rubber band and bulging with cash.

"Oh God!" I sob. "Gary! How could you?"

He walks over to my side and puts his arm around me and turns me to him.

"It's only dope," he says.

"*Now* it is!" I cry. "But the next thing you know, it'll be cocaine!"

"No!" he says. "It won't!"

He almost shouts it.

"I sell dope," he says. "And only dope. And just from now until the end of the summer.

"I wouldn't go near coke," he says. "Or crack. Or anything like that. I swear! I've seen too many kids—and too many grown-ups—back in Scarsdale. I *know* what serious drugs do to people. I've *seen* it. I've seen people wreck themselves with coke. I wouldn't get within ten thousand miles of the stuff. Not for a million dollars. I swear!!"

"But why do it at all?" I ask him.

"I need the money!" he says.

"Why?" I ask him. "To buy me a video camera?!"

"No!"

"Then why?" I ask him. "What would your father say if he knew?"

Gary just looks at me for a second and then, throwing back his head, he breaks out laughing.

"He'd probably shake my hand," he says, "and congratulate me on being a chip off the old block."

I don't get it. I don't get what Gary's saying or understand why he's laughing. But it doesn't matter.

"You've got to quit," I tell him. "Right now. Promise me. Promise me you'll quit."

Gary stops laughing and looks me in the eye and shakes his head and says, "I can't."

And then, without waiting for me to ask him why he can't, he turns to the fireplace and reaches out to the safe-storage box and slides it back into place.

As the drawer clicks shut, I say, "Why can't you?"

Gary heaves a sigh and then, turning back to me, he says, "Because . . . Oh, shit! Can't you just trust me that I can't?"

"No!" I tell him. "Because you *have to!*"

He looks at me.

"Or . . . ?" he says.

"Or . . ." I begin.

I don't want to say it. But I don't have to because Gary looks at me and, as if he can't believe it, he says, "You'd stop going out with me?"

I nod and say, "Yes."

Gary winces and closes his eyes as if I'd hit him hard and hurt him badly.

I feel terrible. I don't want to hurt Gary. I love him. But I hate what he's doing, and he's got to stop it.

"It's too awful!" I tell him. "It's dirty! It makes *you* dirty!"

Gary opens his eyes and looks at me and shakes his head.

"I don't see it that way," he says.

"I'm telling you how *I* see it!" I tell him. "How it makes me feel! If you're that broke, why don't you get a job?"

Gary shakes his head.

"I couldn't make enough."

"For what?"

Gary doesn't answer. He just heaves a sigh and turns away from me and looks down at the floor and shakes his head. And then, after a second, in a voice hoarse with held-back tears, he says, "Look, there's something you ought to know about me."

As he turns back to me and lifts his eyes to mine, I see tears streaming down his face.

"About me and my father," he says.

I stand there, saying nothing, waiting for the rest.

Gary takes a deep breath and, like it's the hardest thing he's ever had to say, he says, "I hate my father."

"Gary!"

"No," he says.

He shakes his head and tries to collect himself. But he can't stop crying. He can't hold back his tears.

"Everything I told you," he says, "everything I told you he did—the aerobic dance studios, the dinner theatre, the home improvement association he started in Massachusetts—they all went bust. All of them.

"My father's never made a go of anything. Not once in his whole life.

"But that hasn't stopped him. He's just gone on to bigger and bigger deals and gotten deeper and deeper into doing business with worse and worse people.

"The reason his partner dropped out of this place

215

is he got sent to prison—for extortion and fraud. Nice, huh?

"That's when my mother finally got out. When Johnny Doyle got sent to Allendale. Up until then, she didn't know where my father was getting his money from.

"I guess my father had gone into business with some pretty shady characters before. But Johnny Doyle was lower than she was willing to go.

"You wonder why I'm so good at dancing with Van Dyke? Because I've had lots of practice. That's why.

"Me and my mother, we've been dodging bill collectors and ducking city marshals and dancing with cops for as long as I can remember.

"I've lived in six different states since I was ten. My father can't even go back to two of them. They'd arrest him.

"Can you imagine what it's like? Growing up with a father like that? Can you imagine how you'd feel, if your father was a cheap hustler who was swindling his neighbors—your friends' parents—out of their money? Out of their dreams?

"It's a killer! Believe me! It makes you feel like shit!"

"Oh Gary!" I say. "I'm so sorry."

"So," he says, "I made up my mind a long time ago. That's not how it's going to be for my kids. My kids are going to have a father who they don't have to lie for. A father who they can be proud of. A father who contributes something. Something of value.

"I'm smart," he says. "And I'm not afraid of hard work."

He laughs.

"And if there's one thing my father's taught

me," he says, "it's the difference between right and wrong.

"I'm not like my father," he says. "I'm going to do it the right way. I'm going to college. And I'm going to get myself a degree and a marketable skill. And I'm going do something with my life. Something good and something big."

"College?" I say. "I thought you wanted to be a rock star."

"Come on," he says. "You know the odds on that."

"You can be anything you want to be," I remind him.

He laughs and shakes his head.

"I'm not that big a dreamer," he says. "I've got to be realistic. I can't plan on getting lucky. I've got to work my way to the end of the rainbow.

"And I don't expect anybody to help me," he says. "So I've got to help myself.

"This dope thing . . ."

He shakes his head.

"I wouldn't do it if I didn't absolutely have to. I swear!

"But I think I'm going to get into Columbia. They've got me wait-listed. But whether it's Columbia or N.Y.U. or wherever, it isn't going to be cheap.

"But if it's Columbia, like I'm hoping, I've got a friend—a guy I knew back in Scarsdale—who goes there and runs a student laundry. And if I can get ten thousand dollars together by September, I can buy into it. And then," he says, "if I work nights and weekends, I can earn my money back and pay my way through school. Maybe even go on to graduate school. Maybe be a lawyer. An environmental lawyer."

217

He laughs.

"Then I could bring a suit to tear down Waterford Village Estates and put up a nice open field in its place. Waterford Meadows!"

He laughs again and looks at me. His face is streaked with tears.

"So, that's why," he says. "That's where the twenty-five bucks I make on every ounce of grass that I sell goes. To the Waterford Meadows Fund.

"I wish . . ." he says. "Oh, shit!"

He reaches out to me and pulls me to him and holds me close.

"I'm sorry, Angelica," he says. "If I've made you feel ashamed or . . ."

He leans back from me and—while tears continue streaming down his face—he says, "I love you, Angelica. You're the best thing in my life. The only really good thing. If I lost you . . ."

There are tears streaming down my face too. I'm aching to stop this, to kiss Gary and tell him that he'll never lose me, that I'll love him forever, as I love him now.

But I'm so confused. And so upset. And so afraid.

"Do you promise you'll be careful?" I ask him.

"I swear!" he says.

"And you'll never sell anything but—"

"Marijuana," he says. "I swear!"

"I love you, Gary. I hate what you're doing. I hate that you have to. But I love you so much . . ."

"You won't leave me?"

"I couldn't," I tell him. "Ever."

"Oh, babe . . ." he says. And he kisses me. And

he lifts me in his arms. And he wraps my legs around his waist.

And he eases us down to the mattress. And loves me. Slow and strong. Like he's never loved me before.

Forty

I'm dancing. I'm barefoot and wearing a silk negligee with a lace bodice and a fitted waist and a skirt that falls straight from my hips and lifts off the floor as I whirl.

I'm all alone, but I'm so happy.

Somewhere in the distance, I hear a phone ringing, but I don't want to stop. I want to keep on dancing, just like this.

"I'll get it."

Gary!

I open my eyes. I'm in Gary's house, in Gary's bedroom, in the bed that Gary bought us, especially for tonight, wearing the silk negligee that Gary bought me, especially for tonight, because tonight is the night of Gary's senior prom and the first night that we've ever spent together.

My mother thinks we're at a chaperoned beach party out at the lake, and she doesn't expect me home before dawn, which it isn't yet.

It's the middle of the night. Except for the moonlight, pouring through the window and stretching across the floor, Gary's room is pitch black.

We didn't leave the prom until after midnight because we were having so much fun.

I'd almost forgotten how well Gary danced and

how dancing with him was the next best thing to making love.

Gary looked so great in the white dinner jacket and cummerbund that he rented to wear with his best jeans. And he said that I looked fabulous in the floor-length, pale blue satin, off-the-shoulder sheath that I'd bought myself just for the occasion.

But anyway, with the prom and then the trip to the lake, where we put in a brief appearance at the chaperoned beach party—checking in noisily and then slipping out quietly—we didn't get back here until after one o'clock.

And then . . .

Oh, God . . .

Making love . . .

And then . . .

Oh, God . . .

God . . .

Making love again . . .

I sigh out loud and stretch and smile and tell myself, *It's got to be at least three o'clock in the morning.*

The house is so quiet. Over the hum of the air conditioner and the murmur of the radio, playing soft music in the corner of the room, I can hear Gary, out in the living room, talking on the phone. I can't make out what he's saying, but—because of the hour—I guess that he's talking to his father.

I guess that Gary's father is calling him from someplace out west, someplace where it's three hours earlier than it is here.

But now, I can't hear Gary anymore. The conversation has broken off.

I imagine Gary hanging up the phone. I imagine him getting up from the mattress, where he's been sitting as he talked, and walking to the door and stepping into the hallway and heading back this way.

I roll over, so I can see him when he walks through the door.

He'll be naked, I think. *And in the moonlight, he'll be beautiful.*

I'm not wrong. As Gary walks in the door, he's both.

I start to smile at the sheer pleasure of seeing him this way—as no one else sees him—but as Gary walks toward the bed, I see the troubled look on his face and I realize that something's wrong. No longer smiling, I whisper, "Gary?"

The sound of my voice startles him. He looks at me, as if he'd forgotten I was here.

"Is something wrong?" I ask him.

Gary nods.

"There's been an accident," he says.

He sits down on the bed beside me.

"Brian Avery," he says.

I know it's something awful. I know that something awful has happened to Brian. But I'm too afraid to ask what.

Gary saves me the trouble. He reaches over and takes my hand and, speaking just above a whisper, he says, "He's dead."

I hear myself, inside my head, screaming, *No! It can't be! You've got it wrong!*

But Gary doesn't hear the screaming in my head.

"Somewhere out past Henderson Harbor," he says. "They found his car turned over in a ditch. The wheels were still spinning when the first state trooper got there. But it was already too late."

"Oh, God!" I cry. "What about Pamela?"

"They've got her at Good Samaritan Hospital," he says.

He shakes his head.

"They don't know if she'll make it."

"Jesus, God!"

"I know," says Gary. "It's awful!"

I throw back the sheet and start to climb out of bed, but Gary grabs my arm and holds me.

"Where are you going?"

"To the hospital," I tell him.

"Why?"

"I don't know," I tell him. "To be there."

I try to pull free of his grip, but he tightens his hold on me.

"No!" he says—like it's a command, like it's an *order!*

I look at him.

"Why not?"

He heaves a sigh.

"I might as well tell you," he says. "It will be all over the papers tomorrow."

"What?"

"They found a packet of white powder on him," he says. "On Brian. In one of his pockets."

I guess I'm supposed to know what that means, and maybe I do, but I don't say anything.

I wait for Gary to say it and, after a second, he does.

"They think it might be cocaine," he says.

It happens in less than an instant. In less than an instant—faster than I can think and with a terrible clarity—everything falls into place.

In one blinding flash, I know where Brian got the cocaine that killed him. I know that he got it from Gary. And I know if I ask Gary about it, he'll tell me it isn't so. He'll lie to me!

Because whatever else he is, however much I love

him, even though it kills me to admit it, I know that Gary Everson is a liar!

Right from the beginning when he lied to my mother about owning a TV, right up to the end when he lied to me about never selling anything but marijuana, everything that Gary's ever told me— about his father, about his mother, about himself, about me, loving me—all of it was lies!

How could I have believed him? Did I need his love so desperately? Couldn't I see that Gary could never love anybody but himself? Never care about anybody but—

"Liar!"

I scream it at the top of my lungs and swing at Gary and slap him across the face, as hard as I can.

"Murderer!"

I scream again and swing again and slap him again, even harder than before.

"Bastard!"

I sob and hang my head.

I haven't the strength to slap Gary again. I haven't the strength to go on living. I haven't the strength to do anything but just sit there, sobbing and wishing that I could die.

But then, after a moment, Gary reaches out and takes my chin in his hand and raises my eyes to his.

He looks bewildered—like he can't believe it—as he says, "You don't think that Brian got his coke from—?"

"Stop it!" I shout.

"He didn't!" Gary insists.

"You didn't sell it to him?"

"I swear!" he says.

I know he's lying, just as I knew he'd lie.

I look him in the eye and say, "Show me."

224

"What?" he says, as if he doesn't know what I'm talking about.

"Your stash," I tell him.

He looks hurt, insulted.

"You don't believe me?" he says.

"I'll look for myself," I tell him.

And I start to climb out of bed again, but again, Gary grabs my arm and holds me. "I warned him," he says.

I look at him.

"But you know Brian," he says. "He's—"

"Liar!" I shout.

And I lash out at him and slap him hard across the mouth. And now, finally, I see tears in Gary's eyes. But it's too late for tears, his or mine.

"I didn't want to do it," he says. "I didn't want to sell coke. Not to Brian or anybody else. But my supplier insisted. 'One time only,' he said. 'Just for prom night.' He figured there'd be a big demand for it. We'd make a lot of money, fast."

"You did it for the *money?*" I ask him.

I can't believe it.

Gary shakes his head.

"No," he says.

"Why didn't you just tell your supplier to go to hell?" I ask him.

"I *couldn't!*" he says. "I *can't!*"

"Why not?" I ask him.

"You don't want to know," he says.

"I do!" I insist.

Gary shakes his head.

"I'm sorry," he says.

He won't tell me. But it doesn't matter. If he *did* tell me, it would probably be a lie, like all the others, and I couldn't stand another lie. It's time the truth came out, past time.

225

"You have to go to the police."

Gary smiles and shakes his head.

"They'd arrest me," he says.

"Yes," I say. "You and your supplier."

Still smiling, Gary says, "No. They won't arrest my supplier. And they won't arrest me either. By this time tomorrow, I'll have turned everything back over to my supplier. There won't be anything here that can tie me in with Brian or drugs or anything else."

"And that will be that?" I ask him.

Gary nods.

"Until when?" I ask him. "Until after Brian's funeral? Or Pamela's? How many more people have to die before you stop?"

"There's nothing I can do," says Gary.

"Well," I tell him, "there's something *I* can do."

He looks at me.

"If *you* won't go to the police," I tell him, "*I* will!"

Gary smiles and shakes his head and says, "No, you won't."

"Don't count on it," I tell him.

"I do," he says.

He puts his hand on my shoulder and looks me in the eye.

"You're mad at me, now," he says. "I understand that. But a just little while ago . . ."

"Don't!" I shout.

I shrug his hand off my shoulder.

"Don't remind me," I tell him. "Whatever happened, you've got to know . . ." I take a deep breath. "I hate you, Gary!"

"No," he says.

"I think you're the worst piece of shit I've ever met."

He looks at me.

"I don't know how I let you fool me into thinking you were anything else," I tell him. "But you did. And I hate you for that too."

"I love you," he says.

I pretend he didn't.

"I'm going home now," I tell him. "And in the morning, I'm going to the police."

I start to climb out of bed, but Gary grabs my arm and looks into my eyes.

"They already know," he says.

"What?"

He heaves a sigh.

"Who do you think called me just now?" he says.

"Who?"

"Van Dyke."

"Van Dyke?"

"He's my supplier."

"Van Dyke?!"

Gary nods.

"Last summer," he says, "when I first got here, I brought a little dope with me, and one morning when I was going out exploring, I rolled a joint for the trip.

"I walked up through the woods and got to the quarry. It seemed like a good place to light up. I didn't know how close I was to the road. Or that the cops were always checking the place out to make sure there weren't any kids swimming in the pond or whatever it is—the water hole.

"So I sat down. And lit up. Then, the next thing I know, I hear somebody behind me saying, 'Freeze!'

"I look around, and there's Van Dyke, pointing his gun at me. Like I'm a crook or an escaped convict or something.

"He could have arrested me, right there. Handcuffed me and thrown me in jail. But instead, after we'd talked awhile and he'd figured out who I was and, you know, how smart I was and everything, he offered me a deal, which—under the circumstances—I couldn't refuse.

"He told me he might see his way clear to letting me go, if I'd go to work for him—selling dope that he'd supply. He'd give me twenty-five dollars off the top of every ounce I sold and he'd take the rest.

"It seemed like a pretty good deal at the time. I mean, not going to jail. And getting a chance to make some money to live on and for school. And all I had to do was peddle a little dope to a few kids who I thought could handle it.

"It didn't work out that way of course. Because Van Dyke got hold of some coke. Over a pound of it. And one night last week he brought it over here and handed it to me.

"I told him I didn't want to sell it. I told him I wouldn't. But he asked me if I'd rather go to jail.

"Isn't that great? I mean, he could have busted me right there for dealing the coke that he'd brought me. My fingerprints were on the bag! He could have said it was mine and busted me and made it stick. He could have sent me to prison for *twenty years!* So . . ."

He shrugs his shoulders and looks at me like he hopes I'll understand, like he hopes I'll sympathize with him.

"You should have let him arrest you," I tell him. "The first time. Up in the quarry. What could they have done to you? All you had was a joint."

"And a record," he says.

I look at him.

"When we lived in Marblehead," he says. "I got busted."

"For selling drugs?" I ask him.

"Marijuana," he says. "I got a suspended sentence. But this would have been my second offense. I would have gone to prison."

"You should have," I tell him. "If you had, Brian Avery would still be alive."

"I know," he says. "I can't tell you how sorry I am."

"Sorry isn't good enough," I tell him. "It's got to stop. Before more kids die. Somebody's got to stop it."

Gary shakes his head.

"Not me," he says.

I look him in the eye.

"If *you* don't," I tell him. "*I* will."

Gary grins.

"I don't believe that," he says.

I start to climb out of bed.

Gary grabs my arm. But this time, I tear my arm away from him and jump out of bed and gather up my clothes and head for the door.

"Angelica?"

I stop in the doorway and turn back and look at Gary.

He hasn't moved. He's still sitting on the bed. There are tears streaming down his face as he says, "I love you, Angelica."

There are tears streaming down my face as I say, "Tough shit."

I turn my back on him. I step through the doorway and I'm gone.

Forty-one

Pamela died between four and five A.M. I heard it on the five o'clock news. I was listening on the radio in my room. I wasn't worried about waking my mother because she wasn't home.

She probably figured, since she didn't expect me home before dawn anyway, it was a good night for her to work late with David Manion.

But when she pulls the car in the driveway, it's a little after five-thirty, and I'm waiting for her in the kitchen.

As she lets herself in the back door and sees me sitting at the kitchen table, she's more embarrassed than surprised. Right away, instead of asking me what I'm doing home, like you'd expect her to, she tells me where she's been. She tells me she's been working late with David Manion.

But I can see that she's been drinking. Her eyes are glistening, like they do when she drinks, and there are roses in her cheeks.

I guess, if it wasn't for everything that's happened in the last twenty-four hours, I probably wouldn't say anything. But suddenly, with everything that's happened to Pamela and Brian, to Gary and me, I've lost my appetite for pretending.

So I tell my mother, as nicely as I can, that it used to bother me a lot that she and David Manion were lovers, but that I understand it better now, and it's okay, she doesn't have to make up stories to hide it from me anymore.

I don't know how I expect her to react. The truth is, I haven't thought about it.

I guess I should expect her to be furious, to fly into a rage and deny everything. But she doesn't do anything like that.

For a second, when I've finished, she just stands there and looks at me. And then, as tears come to her eyes, she kind of smiles and shakes her head and says, "Oh, baby, I'm so sorry."

And the next thing I know, the two of us are standing in middle of the kitchen, hugging each other and crying.

After a while, when we've both had a good cry, we pull ourselves together.

My mother puts up a pot of coffee and when it's ready, we sit down at the kitchen table and she tells me about her and David Manion, how they went from being a boss and his secretary to being good friends and how—without either of them really wanting it to at first, but gradually, over the months and years—their friendship turned into something else.

It's hard to give a name to what their relationship has turned into, she tells me, although she's sure that the town gossips wouldn't have any trouble finding words to describe it. But she wants me to know that it's a loving relationship.

David Manion, she tells me, is a very good man, who loves her very much. And in a way, she tells me, she loves him too—although not in the way that she loved my father. He was and always will be the one great love of her life.

"But a lifetime is a very long time," she tells me.

"Not for everyone," I say. I'm thinking about Pamela Rush and Brian Avery.

My mother looks at me.

"I'm sorry," I tell her. "I was thinking about something else. I'm sorry. I'm glad you have someone in your life. Someone who loves you. I really am. I mean it.

"But I can't talk about it anymore now," I tell her. "There's something I have to do."

"What?" she asks me.

"I don't know yet," I tell her. "But something has to be done, and I'm probably the only one who can do it."

"What is it?" she asks me.

"I don't know yet. I haven't figured it out yet. But I have to do it soon," I tell her. "And when I do, I may need your help."

She doesn't know what I'm talking about and I don't either. But for once, it doesn't seem to matter. Reaching across the table, she takes my hand and says, "You've got it."

Forty-two

It's now seven forty-five. I'm lying in the weeds about fifty yards from Gary's house. I'm at the side of the house, so I can see both the front and back doors.

I'm hoping that Gary didn't pick up his cap and gown early. I'm hoping that he'll be going in to school to get his cap and gown when all the other seniors get theirs—the first thing this morning.

If he does, I've got a plan, a plan that I came up with about an hour ago, a plan that will put Gary and his supplier out of business.

The first part of the plan is the hardest, even though it should take under five minutes to execute.

It better take under five minutes to execute! I think. *If I really have five minutes.*

Gary's back door swings open. I pick up my binoculars. They used to be my father's. I focus on Gary's back door.

Gary walks out onto his back porch. The minute I see him, I feel this terrible rush of love for him. Still. In spite of everything.

But I tell myself, *Too bad.* And I watch, as Gary locks his back door, and I follow him with my binoculars as he walks over to his father's car, and I watch as he climbs into the car and starts up, and I follow him as he drives off.

Before Gary reaches the end of the street, I let go of the binoculars and reach beside me and pick up a good-sized rock.

As he stops at Eastern Boulevard and then disappears around the corner, I push myself up to my knees and, with my free hand, I grab my backpack.

I feel the weight of the rock in my hand and the tug of the binoculars dangling from my neck, as I spring to my feet and take off, running across the field and heading for Gary's back door.

Forty-three

I expect to hear a shrill siren or a clanging bell, but as I smash the window in Gary's back door, I hear nothing but the tinny clatter of glass, falling to the floor on the other side of the door.

Nonetheless, as I reach through the broken window and find the doorknob and open the door from the inside, I can hear the alarm sounding at the police station, downtown.

I can see the police officer on duty switching on his radio and alerting the patrol cars. *Burglary in progress at Waterford Village Estates. All cars respond.*

I can see Van Dyke responding to the call, slamming his patrol car into gear, flooring it and digging out.

Will he sound his siren? I wonder. *Will I hear him coming to get me? Coming closer and closer?*

I shove the thought out of my mind. I don't have time for it. I have just five minutes.

Racing through Gary's kitchen, I run into the living room and over to the fireplace.

Suddenly, as I stand before the fireplace, it occurs to me that Gary might have lied to me about Van Dyke's picking up his stash today. He could have picked it up last night. The safe-storage box could be empty.

I grab the handle for the flue. I push it in. I hear the dull clank of the shutter, opening. I put my fingers on the bottom edge of the handle and push it straight up and feel it slide into its housing. Holding the handle in, I slide it six inches to the left and then bring it back, slowly, halfway to— *click*—the two fieldstones pop out from under the mantel. I reach beneath them and slide out the drawer.

It's all there. Dope, cigarette papers, scale, money and—in a big plastic baggie—about half a pound of white powder.

Cocaine! I think. I freeze at the sight of it. But not for long.

I grab it. I grab everything and, as I stuff it all into my backpack, I'm already heading back the way I came. Racing back through the kitchen, I swing my backpack onto my back and run out the back door.

As I hit the field behind Gary's house, I keep running, running diagonally across the field, racing for the first line of trees at the edge of the field, but keeping my eyes on the corner at Eastern Boulevard, so I can spot the police cars as they come around the corner. I don't make it as far as the trees.

I see the flashing red lights of a police car tearing along Eastern Boulevard and—just before it hits the corner—I dive, flat out, into the tall grass, just a few feet short of the trees.

For a second, I lie there, not moving, scared out my wits, and fighting for my breath. Behind me, I hear the squeal of tires as the police car skids to a stop.

A second later, I hear the slam of the car door. Moving very carefully, I slide around and part the

236

grass in front of me and peek out across the field to Gary's house.

At first I don't see anything, not even the police car, which is probably parked in the driveway at the front of the house. But then, after a minute, I see Van Dyke, walking around the side of the house.

As he gets to the back of the house, Van Dyke sees the back door. It's open, the way I left it, with the glass broken out of the window.

The second he sees it, Van Dyke flattens himself against the back of the house and takes out his gun. And then, slowly, as I watch from my hiding place in the grass, he begins inching his way over toward the open door.

When he's only a couple feet away, he stops and shouts, "Okay, in there!"

He sounds scared.

"It's over!" he shouts. "Throw out your weapons and come out with your hands up! Now!"

He waits.

No one answers.

He glances around the field at the back of the house.

I duck my head as his eyes sweep over me.

"You've got thirty seconds!" he shouts.

I look up.

Van Dyke isn't waiting any thirty seconds. He's already on the move. Crouching low, he runs toward the door and dives through it.

The second his body disappears through the doorway, I jump to my feet and run for the trees and the covering shelter of my old friend—the country at the edge of town.

Forty-four

At nine forty-five, Gary pulls up in front of my house. I've been sitting by the window in my mother's bedroom, sitting at her desk and waiting for him. I get up from the desk and hurry downstairs.

I get to the front door and, before Gary has a chance to ring the bell, I open it.

"Where is it?"

It's the first thing he says.

I tell him, "It's gone."

"Come on!" he says. "This is serious!"

"Would you like to come in?" I ask him.

I step back and open the door for him.

He steps inside the house.

I close the door and walk into the living room.

He follows after me.

"If I don't have everything there when Van Dyke comes around to pick it up, my ass will be grass," he says. "You know that, don't you?"

I sit down in a chair by the window.

"You must have saved a lot of money," I say, "since last summer. Why don't you just give it to him?"

"That's my future!" he tells me.

"What about Brian's future?" I ask him. "And Pamela's? Have you thought about that?"

He walks over and stands in front of me.

"Look," he says. "I've told you how sorry I am about that. If I could change it, if I could make it so it didn't happen, I would. But I can't! I've got to worry about me, now. If I don't come up with the money that I owe Van Dyke and with the rest of the coke and the dope . . ."

He shakes his head.

"He's going to beat the shit out of me, just for starters," he says. "And then, if he doesn't kill me, he's going to figure out a way to put me away for a long time. I'm not kidding!"

"Neither am I," I tell him.

"Van Dyke's not a guy you fuck around with," he says.

"I'll keep that in mind," I tell him.

"Give me my drugs, Angelica!" he says, like *he's* not a guy you fuck around with either.

"Give me my money!" he says. "I mean it!"

"I don't have your money," I tell him. "Or your drugs."

"Bullshit!" he shouts.

"I put them where they belong," I tell him.

He looks at me. It's finally beginning to dawn on him.

"Where?" he asks me. But he's already guessed.

"Down the toilet," I tell him.

"No!!" he wails.

"What are you going to do?" I ask him.

"The money, too?"

"Everything," I tell him. "What I couldn't flush, I took downstairs to the boiler and burned."

"You've fuckin' *killed me!!*" he says.

"You could run away," I suggest. "You could just hop into your car and take off."

He looks at me. He's in total shock. "Where am I supposed to go?" he ask me.

"Where does your father go?" I ask him.

He snarls at me.

"I'm not my fucking father!"

"That remains to be seen," I tell him.

He looks like he's about to cry.

"What am I going to do?" he says.

I smile and say, "I thought you'd never ask."

Forty-five

Twilight. Eight o'clock sharp. A car turns the corner at Eastern Boulevard and cruises down the street. It's a police car.

It turns into Gary's driveway and pulls to a stop. Officer Glenn Van Dyke climbs out from behind the wheel. He reaches back into the car and brings out an athletic bag with a Nike logo printed on its side. He carries the bag up the path that leads to Gary's door, climbs Gary's front steps, and rings the bell.

Inside the house, in his living room, Gary reaches inside his ice chest and switches on his cassette recorder. He puts the cover on the ice chest and a pile of books and papers on top of that. He glances toward the window at the side of the house and then, as Van Dyke rings the doorbell again, he gets to his feet.

"Coming!" he calls.

He goes to the door.

A moment later, as Gary leads Van Dyke into his living room, I lift my video camera to my shoulder and—shooting through the window at the side of the house—I begin taping.

As he reaches the center of the room, Gary stops and turns to Van Dyke.

Van Dyke drops the athletic bag at Gary's feet.

Gary looks at the bag.

241

Van Dyke tells him to hurry up, he hasn't got all day.

Gary doesn't move. But now, still looking at the bag, he begins talking.

I can't hear what he's saying, but I suppose he's telling Van Dyke that he hasn't got anything to put in the bag.

Van Dyke laughs. And then, grabbing his gun with one hand and the front of Gary's shirt with the other, he yanks Gary to him.

Gary starts to explain, but before he can, Van Dyke smashes his face with the back of his hand.

Gary cries out as he falls to the floor.

Van Dyke kicks him.

Gary grunts with the pain and curls up in a ball.

Van Dyke squats down over him. He grabs Gary's hair and lifts his face from the floor. Gary's face is covered with blood.

"I don't know who you think you're playing with, sonny."

I hear Van Dyke loud and clear.

"But if you don't come up with my coke and my smoke and all of my money by midnight tonight, you're dead meat!"

He gets to his feet.

"I'll be back at midnight," he says. "You be here. With all the stuff. Or you're dead meat!"

He kicks Gary again.

Gary cries out.

Van Dyke smiles and shakes his head.

"Have a nice day," he says.

He turns and heads for the door.

As he does, I shut off my video camera and drop down from the window and hide in the shrubs at the side of Gary's house and pray that Van Dyke won't decide to take a look around the house before he leaves.

But after a moment, I hear Van Dyke climbing into his car and starting up. And then I hear him shifting into gear and driving off.

I wait until I can no longer hear the sound of his car, and then, a little longer.

"Angelica!"

I hear Gary calling to me from inside the house.

"Angelica!"

I get to my feet. I'm sopping wet and shaking so bad I can hardly stand up. But I've got that son of a bitch, Van Dyke, right where I want him, and I've never felt better in my life.

Forty-six

Inside the house, I do what I can for Gary. I get him a wet towel for his face, and I help him to his feet.

"What now?" he says.

"We've got an appointment with Agent Patrick B. McMahon of the Federal Bureau of Investigation in two hours," I tell him.

Gary looks at me like I'm crazy.

"Where?" he says.

As I open up Gary's ice chest and turn off his cassette recorder, I tell him, "The Chimes Building, on Salina Street in Syracuse. Room 1601."

As I eject the cassette from the cassette recorder, Gary says, "You called him?"

"He didn't call me," I tell him as I slip the cassette into my pocket.

"You didn't tell him your name, did you?"

I nod and say, "My name, your name, Van Dyke's name—everything."

"Why'd you do that?" he asks me.

"In case something happened to me," I tell him.

"Jesus! You didn't have to go to the FBI," he says. "With your tape and mine, we could have gotten Van Dyke off my back. We could have made him quit. We still can! I mean, what's the FBI got if they don't have the tapes? A crank phone call, right?''

There's a pleading look in Gary's eyes, a look that's hard to ignore, even now. But I manage to.

"I told Agent McMahon that you'd be coming with me," I tell him. "He said that if you did it might help you with the U.S. Attorney and the court."

Gary looks at me. He can't believe it.

"I'll be back for you in fifteen minutes," I tell him. "That will give you time to clean up and change. Don't make me wait, okay?"

I turn and head for the door.

"Angelica?"

I stop at the door.

"Yes?"

"Nothing."

I nod and say, "Fifteen minutes."

And then I let myself out the door.

Forty-seven

When I get to my house, my mother is sitting in the living room, reading a book and sipping a glass of wine.

When I say, "Hello," she looks up at me, and I guess I must look strange—different from the way I normally look—because she looks at me with real concern, and she says, "Are you okay?"

I don't want to tell her everything that's happened. There will be time for that later.

So I tell her that I'm fine, but there's something important I have to do, and then I ask her for a favor.

Forty-eight

As I drive Gary to Syracuse, neither of us has much to say.

We just drive along, listening to the sound of the music playing on the radio and the air rushing past the open windows and the smooth purring of my father's classic '65 Ford Mustang.

BRUCE AND CAROLE HART began writing for television in the late 1960s. They wrote some of the first scripts and songs for "Sesame Street" and also helped put together the Marlo Thomas special, "Free To Be . . . You and Me." They produced, directed, and—with Stephen Lawrence—wrote the songs for the television-movie "Sooner or Later," which was also their first novel. They also created and produced NBC's Emmy-winning series, "Hot Hero Sandwich."

The Harts write for young adults because they feel that "very few authors, filmmakers, television producers, etc., communicate honestly with young people about the important issues in their lives. Too often, this leaves young people feeling isolated, nonexistent, unimportant. It leaves them without a realistic perspective for dealing with their problems. We write to tell them that they are not alone and that what they care about matters very much—to them and to all of us."